Pra

~

Praise for *The Vienna Sketchbook*

"You could describe Meritta Koivisto's historical novel *The Vienna Sketchbook*, first published in 2017, as a forgotten gem... Koivisto carries the story along at a rapid pace, but keeps the tension right to the end... She uses very small tools to say something unbelievably large about how war can change a person."

—Kirsinkirjanurkka

"The book describes in a subtle way how evil begins to manifest itself little by little, with whispers in the corners of apartments and conversations on street corners... Koivisto writes skillfully about a change that no one wanted to believe could happen, and how in the end it changed everything... Koivisto's novel is a moving tale of tragic events."

—Kuohu

"*The Vienna Sketchbook* is an impressive book in many ways... Koivisto writes with great skill and with respect for her readers' intelligence, never explaining too much... *The Vienna Sketchbook* is an enjoyable reading experience in spite of its heavy subject."

—Kirjaluotsi

THE VIENNA SKETCHBOOK

A NOVEL

MERITTA KOIVISTO

Love in the middle of noon
In all the corners of death
Till its shadow will be no more.

—"When The War is Over",
   The Mauthausen Trilogy, Iakovos Kambanellis

PROLOGUE

They woke me up again. The girls' screams. They have never gone completely silent.

A mass grave was found. Someone somewhere decided to build a shopping center in a meadow, and started excavating. Then came heavy rains and flooding, lifting the bones to the surface.

"What happened here, and who these people were, we don't know," the reporter from Austria said on television yesterday evening. In the background churned-up earth, investigators in rain gear, groups of reporters and television cameras.

There were once bluebells and mountain anemones growing in that meadow. And spring water that was crystal clear. And cold. It helped take the worst of the pain out of your hands.

The Ludwig clock on my night table says it's

half past one. I close my eyes. I'm too old, too tired. I've earned my peace. But the night won't grant me peace. I hear the girls scream again and again, an echo reverberating through the treetops. It was summer, 1943. A man's voice splitting the wide blue sky: "Stop!" But the birds flew, and spattered the sky with black.

I

THE COLORS OF VIENNA

Ingria held tight to her sister Margit's whisper-thin veil and tried to match her steps to Papa's stride as he led Margit down the aisle toward the groom.

Ingria was supposed to let go of the veil as soon as Papa stopped to give Margit away to Januck, her husband-to-be. "That's when Margit will step into her new life," her Mama had told her. "Isn't it exciting?"

Ingria thought it would have been much more exciting to go with Januck's little sister Magda to Prater amusement park or Schönbrunn Palace. "Later," her mother had said—to that and to everything else she asked about.

Later.

Ingria roused herself. Sunshine was filtering down through the narrow church window as tiny dust motes danced in the light. Margit stopped and Januck turned to look at her. Papa stood aside and waited. Margit made a little motion and Ingria let go of the veil. It floated like mist and settled at Margit's feet.

Mama's cheeks were red, her white ostrich feather quivering restlessly atop her hat. But Papa smiled reassuringly. Ingria cast her eyes down as she walked over to Papa and took his hand.

~

The wedding reception was at Januck's parents' house—the Waldermanns. Theirs was a small family, Mr. Waldermann said, stroking his walrus mustache. Mrs. Waldermann hardly spoke. No one from her side of the family had come to the wedding. Mama said Mrs. Waldermann's roots were in the Hungarian countryside. Mr. Waldermann was a pharmacist, and most of the guests were people he knew from work, or Januck's classmates from the university.

Ingria sat on a sturdy chair in a corner of the living room, laid her sketchpad down on a table, and examined her drawing. She had finished Margit's headdress. It was like a crown made of icicles, its veil cascading down like a cloud. Margit takes after Mama, Ingria mused. They both have light brown hair and a pointy nose and they both cry easily. Ingria was more like her father. She had dark blue eyes and light, curly hair. But Papa's curls were already turning gray at the temples.

She heard a conversation over at the table where the coffee was. "All the way from Vyborg, in Finland?

You've got quite a long and difficult journey behind you, Mrs. Silo, and another one going back," a woman said as the coffee cups clinked against their saucers and the cake knife clicked against the platter.

"Yes, but there's nothing we wouldn't do for love. Isn't that right, Margit?" Mama said in her thick accent. Margit was sitting on the sofa, beautiful as a bride of the snow. She nodded. Papa just smiled where he sat next to Mama. Ingria knew that Papa hadn't wanted to come to Vienna. Not now, he'd said, reading the paper and looking worried.

"You speak good German, Mrs. Silo," someone said, and Mama said,"Thank you very much. Better French, though. My grandmother was an emigrant from France."

"Is that so?"

Ingria looked around. Where were Januck and his little sister Magda?

She picked up her pad and walked into the foyer. As she started up the stairs, she heard low men's voices on the other side of the front door. One of the people speaking was Januck, her sister's new husband. His voice sounded strange and frantic."I just got word that in the name of racial hygiene the Nazis have started sterilizing Romani girls as young as 14 in Germany. They're picking them up in towns and villages all over the country. They do the procedure in a van..."

Ingria heard her mother come to the doorway behind her.

"Ingria, go and find Januck," Mama said. "It's time for the music."

Ingria nodded, and continued up the stairs. Just then she heard the front door rattle, and Mama shouted happily,

"There you are, my dear Januck! I was hoping that you and Margit might play a four-handed piece. Would that be too much to ask?"

"Dear Lilja, we will do so with pleasure," Januck said in a warm voice. "Did you have any particular tune in mind?" A moment later *Bei Mir Bist Du Schön* filled the house as he and his classmates sang it in chorus around the piano. Mama glowed with happiness and the other guests were soon heartily joining in on the chorus.

That night as Ingria lay down beside Magda Waldermann in her narrow bed, Magda put her arm around Ingria's neck and said that they were related now. Magda was a year older, so she would be the older sister. That seemed nice to Ingria.

"Do you know what sterilize means?" Magda asked. Her eyes were very close to Ingria's, her breath sweet and warm.

Ingria shook her head.

"What does it mean?" she whispered.

Magda shrugged.

"I don't know. Januck said that they were doing it to girls in Germany."

"I heard that, too."

A sly gleam came into Magda's eyes.

"Let's ask him," Ingria said.

But Magda shook her head vehemently.

"I was hiding behind the door curtain. You walked

right past me and didn't notice anything," Magda said, and burst into laughter. Then she pulled the sheet up over her head and waved her arms, playing ghost. Soon they were rolling around on the bed, nearly choking with laughter.

Then Magda fell asleep, but Ingria was still awake, breathing lightly, silently, as if she feared she would awaken that strange word whose meaning she didn't understand. She turned and looked straight into the face of the girl sleeping beside her. The house creaked in the silence. Ingria pressed closer to Magda's warm body and shut her eyes tight.

She slipped into an uneasy dream. In the dream, Nelli, their parlor maid back home, came running in through the garden gate with a letter in her hand and Ingria left her spruce cone cows in the grass and ran after Nelli and tried to take the letter from her, snatching at it again and again, because she knew it was a letter from Januck. Then Nelli's hair suddenly spread out and covered Ingria's face so she couldn't breathe. She started awake, panting, and sat up in bed.

THE FOREST MAIDENS

The next morning after breakfast the house was quiet. Magda had gone to school, Januck was at his medical school lecture, and Ingria's Mama was in her room reading a book about Mahler. Her Papa had gone to the medical wholesalers' with Mr. Waldermann, who wanted to order some supplies for his pharmacy. Mrs. Waldermann was out grocery shopping.

That left just Ingria and Margit.

Ingria sat in the living room and paged through her sketchpad until she came to the picture of the forest maidens.

She had drawn it after the maidens appeared to her and Margit. She and her sister had been wending their way home through a field, threading wild strawberries onto a piece of straw, when Margit suddenly said, "Look!" and pointed into the woods. The forest looked enchanted at that moment, the light refracting through the dark spruce trees like silver mist.

"The forest maidens," Margit said. "Their veils are trailing on the ground. Can you see them?"

Ingria nodded. "Are they the spirits of maidens?"

But just then they heard cowbells clanging and saw horned heads emerge from the rustling underbrush, and the two of them laughed and sprinted home.

The drawing was unfinished, because it was hard to imagine the maidens' faces. But the trees and the shadows were there, and the rays of light peeping from above and touching the soft mounds of moss, and the tiny, sharp leaves of the lingonberry twigs.

"Guten Morgen, liebling," Margit said in a bright, cheerful voice as she came through the heavy velvet curtains.

"Are we supposed to speak German?" Ingria asked.

"No, little one," Margit answered with a smile, and hugged her.

Back at home, Margit had wanted them to speak German at coffee and meal times, and their housekeeper Emma had served the food without speaking, her mouth a tight line, like a stretched rubber band, because she sometimes couldn't understand what they wanted from her. When that happened, Ingria would whisper a Finnish translation. Papa thought they should give up this act, but Mama thought Margit's suggestion was an excellent idea. And now Ingria was glad that she had learned the language well and that her big sister had quizzed her on her German homework for the whole semester, because how else would she have made friends with Magda?

Margit sat down next to her. Ingria could smell her soft scent; it reminded her of summer. The lilies of the valley they picked in the woods.

Ingria showed her the drawing.

"Remember?"

"I remember."

"Are there forest maidens in Austria, too?" Ingria suddenly wanted to know.

"Yes. They're everywhere," Margit said with a laugh.

She's always in a good mood these days, Ingria thought. "Are they spirits?"

"Yes sweetheart, they are. The spirits of girls who died for love."

"Why do they only appear at sunset?" Ingria asked.

"They turn a light toward the darkness, so that people won't lose their way," Margit said somberly.

"Lose their way to where?"

"Oh, sweetheart. You're much too little to understand."

Just then Januck appeared in the doorway. "Understand what?"

But Margit just smiled.

ECHO

They were going into town today, because Mama had a burning desire to hear Mahler. Ingria felt a confused excitement as she watched the bustle of the city, the fashionable people hurrying past, the river of black automobiles, the ornate buildings unlike any she had seen in Vyborg.

"There it is," Mama said happily when she recognized the concert hall.

From a distance, the Musikverein looked to Ingria like an old aunt whose smile had died. As they started to climb the steps, they saw a tag attached to the old aunt's lapel, a sign that said: **Concert Cancelled**.

"Why on earth?" Mama cried.

Then Mrs. Waldermann asked in a low voice, glancing at her husband,

"Do you think they cancelled it because Mahler is Jewish, and Hitler...?"

"That barbarian!" Mama snapped, and Mr. Waldermann looked around nervously.

In the end they decided to go to Café Central for apple strudel.

On the way there they had to walk along the edge of the street because the sidewalk was crowded with people standing in line for something. Januck explained to Margit that they were waiting to get into the office that had been set up to handle Jews leaving the country.

Magda saw a girl from her drawing class, and waved. The girl was named Hadar, and she had thick, curly hair and dimples. Hadar waved enthusiastically back. "Where are they going?" Ingria asked. Mr. Waldermann turned and gave her a stern look. Magda whispered in her ear that Januck had a lot of Jewish friends who were moving away because they'd been fired from their jobs because the Nazis didn't like them. "Why?" Ingria asked, but Magda shrugged her shoulders and rolled her eyes. A car approached from behind them, tooting its horn, and Magda pulled Ingria closer to her.

As they passed the restlessly moving queue, the glances that she didn't understand, Ingria felt a pang of homesickness. She thought of the spruce forest near their house with its pond of clear water and its little fish with their open mouths and silly, staring eyes. She thought about Emma, whose mouth would twist into a smile as she worked in the kitchen and listened to

Ingria chatter. Magda took hold of Ingria's hand, as if she sensed her mood. "Let's ask if you can have Hadar's place at drawing class." Ingria didn't know what to think about that idea, but she did want to draw.

When they had settled in around a large corner table at Café Central and the waiter had taken their order and the men were absorbed in newspapers they'd picked up at the door, Lilja glanced at the girls.

"Ingria is going to study at the Finnish Art Society drawing school and then continue her studies either here in Vienna at the arts academy, or better yet at the Académie Julian in Paris. And your daughter? What plans do you have for her?" Lilja asked Mrs. Waldermann. Both girls turned to look at Magda's mother, an ordinary woman from the countryside, so saddled with daily chores that she hadn't given any thought to her daughter's talent and considered her drawing practice merely a kind of play. Mrs. Waldermann looked around in confusion.

"Time will tell, won't it?" Ingria's father Unto said, laying down his newspaper. Mrs. Waldermann nodded, relieved.

"Ellen Thesloff's painting *Echo* is very moving to me. We are from the countryside, too, after all," Lilja continued.

Since Mrs. Waldermann didn't say anything, Ingria's father put his paper down again and shot a look at his wife. Lilja could see the conversation wasn't going anywhere, but couldn't resist adding, "Thesloff, you see, won the bronze medal at the Paris Exposition in 1900."

"Mama," Margit said.

"So, what shall we do for the rest of the day?" Lilja asked with a forced smile. She turned and saw a long-faced man beside her. "Ah! Here's the waiter."

~

A few days later, Ingria held her father's hand as they climbed the broad granite stairs to the main entrance of the Vienna Academy of Fine Arts. Papa was bringing her drawings to Sister Elke, Magda's drawing teacher, for evaluation.

As they walked through the tall doors into the imposing, pillared foyer, Ingria shut her eyes tight and smelled the pungent aroma of paint. She breathed it in greedily as she walked down the vaulted corridor. It was like entering another world, a hidden world where everything outside was wiped away. She felt she could never get enough of it.

"Do you think Sister Elke will let me into the class?" she asked her Papa.

"We'll see," Papa said, then added with his brow a bit furrowed, "She's an old friend of the Waldermanns. And that's a good thing."

Papa knocked on the office door, but it remained closed and there was no sound from within. He looked around in puzzlement.

"We'll take your drawings directly to the rector."

The door opened immediately when he knocked.

Ingria glanced at the short, plump man standing in the doorway. Papa explained that his daughter was hoping to get into Sister Elke's drawing class, and Ingria tried to listen patiently as he told the man that they were staying with Mr. and Mrs. Waldermann, whose daughter Magda was one of Sister Elke's pupils, and that they would be in Vienna for another month. "Both girls are quite talented," Papa concluded. Then the man took the folder Papa handed him, said he would pass it on, and closed the door.

"That was Rector Bauer," Papa said in a respectful voice.

~

"Januck was here before my mother and father were married," Magda said one evening as they sat drawing in Magda's room.

"What do you mean?"

"Haven't you ever noticed that he and I don't really look alike?"

Earlier that day they had sat at the dining table and drawn portraits of Januck as he sat on the sofa reading the paper. Ingria had certainly noticed that Januck was a bit fairer, and even had white streaks in his whiskers and beard. Januck was bright as a whitecurrant, while Magda reminded her of a dark, leathery autumn plum, fruity and juicy under the skin. They had that kind of plum tree at home in Vyborg, at the back of the garden.

"Now that you mention it, you're right,"

Ingria said. But then she and Margit didn't really look alike, either.

"Januck's mother died," Magda said, her voice quivering.

"Really?"

Magda nodded, her eyes wide. "She died from lack of love, because my father loved my mother. And Januck's mother wasted away. Even Januck said so."

Magda dashed over to fetch something from a drawer in the bureau.

"Here," she said. It was a picture of a straight-backed woman with a little boy beside her. Ingria immediately recognized the boy as Januck.

"I told you, didn't I?"

The woman in her high-necked dress looked thin and solemn.

Ingria nodded.

"Remember when Margit and Januck went somewhere right after the wedding?" Magda said.

"They went to get photos taken."

"And then they went to the Grinzing cemetery! I know it for a fact." Since Magda was waiting for her to ask "How?" Ingria asked.

"Because when they came back, Januck's right knee had mud on it. He'd been kneeling at his mother's grave."

Ingria didn't know what to think about these surprising revelations.

Magda went on.

"Januck goes to her grave often. I can show you where it is."

~

One time when the house was empty and Mrs. Waldermann was puttering about making dinner, Magda grabbed Ingria by the hand and led her into the kitchen.

"Mom, can we go to Rosa Schildt's bakery to buy some apple strudels?"

Mrs. Waldermann looked weary as she sliced carrots into a large pot.

"Wait until Januck and Margit get back from their walk," she said, without turning around. Magda gave Ingria a knowing look. "They can go with you."

"I've been to the bakery by myself before, mother. We can take the tram."

Mrs. Waldermann brushed a lock of hair out of her eyes. Her fingers looked red, her skin worn out, like it had little cracks in it.

"Just go and draw for now, or go play."

"Ingria loves apple strudels so much, don't you, Ingria?" Magda said, and gave her a look that gave her no choice but to nod.

"They are good," Mrs. Waldermann murmured to the carrots as she chopped them up.

"Please, Mother?" Magda whined, batting her big brown eyes. Mrs. Waldermann turned around now.

"All right. But you have to promise that you won't go anywhere else and you'll come straight home. And take the tram."

"I promise."

~

Ingria was never allowed to go out alone at home in Vyborg, and she felt a strange excitement as they hopped onto the tram. As they glided past the window of Rosa Schildt's bakery, Magda shot Ingria a triumphant smile.

"There's movies showing at Burgkino," she said. "Maybe we'll go there sometime." And a little later, "This is where we get off." Magda stood up as the tram turned onto a narrow street. "It's not far from here."

FRIEDSHOF GRINZING, the sign said. Such a fitting name for a final resting place: Place of Peace. They walked down the cemetery path past gravestones covered in moss and vines and pale statues of angels until Magda finally came to a stop and put her hand in front of her mouth.

"What did I tell you? He comes here often in the evening."

Beyond the trees and headstones was Januck. All they could see was his profile. He was talking to another man.

"Let's go closer," Magda whispered.

"Let's leave," Ingria hissed back, but Magda wouldn't let go of her hand, pulling her forward.

"Their strategy in Germany is to get the newspapers to write negative things about the Jews so that they can get the people to accept their political plans," Januck was saying. "The whole point of it all is the same: absolute power, so they can control..."

Ingria had never seen Januck so agitated. His face was white pale, and the piece of paper in his hand trembled.

"Let's go," Ingria whispered again, tugging on Magda's dress. But Magda just stared at Januck with an odd, thoughtful look on her face. Ingria remembered that look much later, but at that moment she forgot it immediately when she saw that Margit was there, too, standing in her white coat and her wide-brimmed black hat, staring at a tall headstone, motionless. Was that Januck's mother's grave? And who was Januck talking to?

"In Germany the Nazis are using every sort of new law to try to isolate the Jews and make them powerless. Their excuse, that there's an international Jewish conspiracy, is quite childish, but unfortunately that sort of simple brainwashing has made the public receptive to their attempt at seizing power. Here in Austria we... well, you can read it for yourself," Januck said.

"Your writing is hard to get published in foreign papers."

"We have to try to get America to wake up," Januck whispered.

They saw Januck glance around and open his coat, take a stack of papers out of his pocket, and hand it to the other man.

"We can't let it happen here," the man said, putting the papers in his coat. He was broad shouldered, with his hat pressed down low on his head. There was something angular, four-square about him, Ingria remembered later. The next moment his broad back disappeared down the wooded pathway.

"Let's go," Ingria whispered into Magda's ear. "Quick." She grabbed Magda's hand. "We can't let Januck see us."

As they ran breathlessly down the hill and jumped onto a tram, Ingria thought about apple strudels and Mrs. Waldermann's tired, trusting eyes.

"Mother is easy to fool," Magda said, smiling, pleased with herself.

~

That evening, Ingria knocked timidly on the door to Margit and Januck's room.

After what seemed a long moment, she heard her sister's muted voice:

"Come in."

Ingria noticed that Margit's face was flushed and her blouse was buttoned crooked. Januck walked past with a smile.

"I'm going to get some elderflower juice," he said in a hoarse voice, and disappeared down the hallway.

"Margit," Ingria began falteringly. "I want to ask you something."

"Come here, sweetheart," Margit said, like she used to, taking Ingria into her open arms.

"Magda said that Januck's mother is dead."

"Oh, sweetheart. Is that what's weighing on your mind?"

Ingria breathed in the faint scent of Margit's neck.

How she wished they could go back to last summer—or rather to summertime, all their summertimes together. Back home. To walk with Margit in the woods, watch the light coming down through the dark spruce trees like a silver mist. But now here she was looking into Margit's moist eyes in this strange room surrounded by a weird, frightening world where unknown people talked about mysterious things.

"Januck's mother died when he was just seven years old," Margit said. "She had tuberculosis."

"Tuberculosis?"

"Yeah. The loss of his mother has been a great sadness for Januck. But Mrs. Waldermann has been a good stepmother to him, and taken care of him since he was little. She was their housekeeper. Then she and Mr. Waldermann got married and had Magda." Margit stroked the top of Ingria's head, lingered there. Then she pressed Ingria against her.

Wasted away from lack of love.

It was only later that Ingria understood that Mr. Waldermann's marriage to his housekeeper had driven all of his relatives away, as well as driving his first wife's family away from his son's wedding, and from his son's entire life, really.

"Here she is," Margit said, taking a photo out of a drawer. It was a picture of the same solemn woman, standing next to a younger, thinner Mr. Waldermann.

Before they went to sleep, Ingria and Magda lay side by

side in bed and flipped through their sketchpads in the light of the lamp on the night table. Magda said that their drawing teacher, Sister Elke, was a nun because she had turned away from desire.

"What desire?"

"Desire for men. For a man to touch her."

"Touch her?" Ingria said, looking at Magda in amazement.

"Touch her here," Magda said. She pulled the covers down, lifted her nightshirt, and pointed between her legs.

"Why would that be so desirable?"

"Because it feels good."

"Oh," Ingria said.

"There's a secret spot there. Haven't you ever tried it?"

Ingria hadn't.

"Maybe you don't have one yet," Magda whispered, her eyes wide. But Magda was older than her, after all.

"Come on," Magda said, sliding off the bed.

"Where?" Ingria asked. But Magda just smiled mysteriously and waved for her to follow. As they walked down the quiet hallway, the whole house seemed to be asleep.

Ingria knew that they were heading toward Mr. and Mrs. Waldermann's room. They stopped in front of the door and waited a moment, then they heard a loud wheeze that changed to a low snore. Magda nearly burst out laughing. They continued to the end of the hallway where Magda started up the attic stairs that led to Margit and Januck's door. From inside the room, Ingria heard the muffled creak of bedsprings, the rustle of sheets, and faint moans. Magda gave her a satisfied look, nodding knowingly. When the creak of the springs stopped, Magda took her hand and they hurried back down to their room.

"Do you often listen to them?" Ingria asked, once they were hidden under the thick quilt again.

"My parents? Sometimes. When I'm feeling bored."

A CHOPINESQUE
LONGING

"Can I draw you, Mrs. Waldermann?" Ingria asked from the doorway. She'd been in her room for hours reading her school books and feeling lonely because Margit and Januck had gone on a walk again and Mama had gone out after breakfast to get some eszterhazys from the pastry shop.

"Of course, my child," Mrs. Waldermann said, busily whipping a berry kissel.

Ingria sat down on a chair by the window and drew a few lines on a page of her sketchpad.

"How do you like it here?" Mrs. Waldermann asked after a moment, but she seemed more interested in the runny kissel than in her.

"Very much, thank you."

Mrs. Waldermann added some flour and started beating harder.

"Did you have fun at the amusement park?"

Margit and Januck had taken her and Magda to the Prater amusement park and they'd ridden the ferris wheel, which made her dizzy when they went over the top.

"Yes, it was very fun."

Ingria slid down from the chair and decided to finish the drawing another time. Her lines just weren't going anywhere. When she got to the door, Mrs. Waldermann turned. "Lunch is almost ready. Could you go and see what's keeping your mother?"

"Yes, Mrs. Waldermann," Ingria said. She knew that the pastry shop was just a few blocks away because they had often walked past it. Magda sometimes made faces at the pimply-faced boy who worked there, and every time, he turned red and stared stupidly at her her with big brown eyes.

Ingria could see Mama from a long way off, leaning against the wall of the building with her eyes closed, an ecstatic look on her face, and she didn't have to guess why, because the door to the third floor balcony was open and mournful piano music was drifting out of it.

"Mama, it's me. Where are the eszterhazys?" Ingria said to her mother's trembling eyelids, but Mama just waved her hand lazily toward the pastry shop.

"Do you hear it, Ingria?"

Ingria closed her eyes and the music carried her

to springtime, when the sun melts the ice and it drips from the eaves, bright and beautiful.

"Chopin. The fourth ballade has always been filled with longing for me," Mama said.

"Mama, I miss home."

"I know, chérie. Always remember, Ingria, that longing keeps you going."

When the music went quiet, Mama took a few steps away from the building, looked up with one hand holding her broad-brimmed hat on, and shouted up,

"You there. That was quite delightful. Schönen dank. May I venture to request that you play the waltz in C-sharp minor? That fourth ballade is so terribly sad, especially in these bleak times."

Ingria wished she could sink right into the ground. The door above remained open, but no one appeared. A curtain in another window fluttered and Ingria saw a sharp-nosed man glare out. Then that window went dark and quiet, mute.

"Mama..." Ingria said, taking hold of the skirt of her mother's new dove-grey dress, but Mama just stared up at the balcony.

"Let's go," Ingria said.

"Bitte, bitte," Mama said to the balcony window.

Then something extraordinary happened. It happened so fast that before Ingria or Mama had time to react the yolk of a broken egg was suddenly dripping off Mama's lace-covered hat, running in a long, slimy trickle from the brim, right in front of her eyes.

"What on earth...?" Mama said as another egg struck her, this time right in her round belly.

"Go back where you came from!" someone shouted.

"Let's run, Mama," Ingria whispered.

"I will not run away from Nazis," Mama said just as Ingria heard another egg splat, and her mother bent forward, as if that little blow to her back had caused her to stumble. But she straightened up and strode away as the egg ran slowly down the back of her dress.

"I will bow to art, Ingria, but not to any person," she said.

When they reached the other end of the block and turned onto the Waldermanns' street, Ingria's skirt was dirtied and Mama looked like a dove who had been rolled in glue. But the look in her eyes told nothing.

"I love you, mother," Ingria said in perfect German, without a trace of an accent. Just to be safe. Because walls have ears.

"Mama," her mother corrected her, and said a moment later, "Many thanks, chérie."

THE LINE IS CROSSED

Everyone was clamoring around the table because Mama had made Finnish pancakes for breakfast and Januck's mother had bought some apricot jam and beat some whipped cream to go with them. The crêpes—as Mama called them—were a big hit, thin and lacy along the edges. Ingria was impressed by her mother's skills, and by the way that Papa watched her with loving eyes, because Mama never set foot in the kitchen at home—that was Emma's territory. Maybe she wanted to show Januck's family that Margit would certainly be able to whip up wonderful breakfasts herself once she and Januck moved into their own place, even though at the moment they just billed and cooed and walked around holding hands and gazing into each other's eyes, letting Mrs. Waldermann take care of breakfast, lunch and dinner on her own. To make things worse, the Waldermanns' Czech housemaid had suddenly packed up her things and left just before their foreign houseguests arrived, and Mrs. Waldermann would under no circumstances allow guests to set foot in the kitchen. But this morning Mama had told Papa that she couldn't watch Januck's mother toiling away along any longer, even if she was a tough, husky woman.

"Liebe Ingria, your mother makes wonderful crêpes," Magda said, smiling sweetly at Mama.

"Vielen dank, liebe Magda," Mama replied.

Papa took a large spoonful of whipped cream with a look of satisfaction and Januck put a hand on Margit's shoulder and gazed at her like he was looking at a priceless treasure. Ingria felt as if there were forces that she had no inkling of, forces so powerful that they had brought her here, with Mama, Papa, and Margit, seated around the Waldermanns' table on this spring morning. And somewhere far away Emma was tending the house, the cows were still rustling through the brush summer and winter, the sun sleeping nearly the whole day away beyond the pale edge of the forest. She knew that Emma would have shaken her head at the apricot jam—they always ate their pancakes with strawberry jam at home. But now, of course, they were in Austria.

At some point, when nearly all of Mama's lacy pancakes were eaten and just one was left on the plate and Mama tried to get one person after another to take it, the doorbell rang. They weren't expecting anyone, and everyone looked at each other in almost amused good spirits, questioningly. Then Januck wiped his mouth on his white napkin and got up. Mama looked smilingly at the pancake, as if she simply couldn't wait for someone to put it on their plate.

When Januck returned a moment later, he looked serious. Margit had an uneasy look in her eyes. For a moment no one said anything. Mama was still smiling at the pancake, but the smile seemed to have frozen on her face.

"The Kaufmanns' shop window was defaced. Someone wrote, 'Don't Buy from Jews'", Januck said.

"Why not buy from them?" Ingria asked Papa, but before he could answer, Januck turned to her and it felt like a flash of lightning over a summer lake on a hot, dry day. "There is no reason for it," Januck said. "They haven't done anything except build this country like everyone else."

"Januck, you shouldn't get mixed up in politics," his father said, a dab of whipped cream jiggling on his thick, yellow-gray mustache. "It could lead to—" but before he finished speaking, Mama said, "Who wants the last pancake?"

"To a free and independent Austria," Januck said, putting the pancake on his plate. "Even if Hitler does come with his henchmen and try to interfere in it."

Everyone looked at each other uncomfortably. It felt to Ingria like a shadow had fallen over the table, and the room became like the yard when it suddenly shrinks to a dull, lead gray before a thunderstorm.

"But there's no way that vulgar man could get in power here," Mama said as she sliced her pancake. "This is Vienna. It could only lead to the worst sort of kitsch. Otto von Habsburg will come back from Belgium and everything will turn out all right, won't it?"

"According to my sources, he's already volunteered to serve as chancellor, on one condition," Januck said.

"What condition?" Mr. Waldermann asked, his eyes slightly bulging.

"He wants the workers of Vienna to be armed."

"Good heavens," Mrs. Waldermann whispered.

"Then Hitler will have to decide whether he's willing to spill German blood to occupy our country," Januck said, his face tense.

"We do have the Catholic Church as a safeguard. That's what Sister Elke thinks," Mr. Waldermann murmured.

"You know very well what Hitler thinks of the Catholic Church," Januck said.

"What about the Jews in Vienna? They're people of means, and they're the largest group of German-speaking Jews in Europe. I'm sure they'll have some influence on the course of events. Don't you think?" Mama said, looking around the table. "In a civilized world you can't just let someone do whatever they want, after all."

"That is a possibility. The Jews here have a lot of money," Mr. Waldermann muttered, not looking at anyone, and he sounded to Ingria devoid of all passion. Maybe it had died with his first wife.

"How did that work out in Germany?" Januck said, but the question seemed to go past his father, whose jaw continued to move with his drooping mustache as he chewed up his pancake. Mr. Waldermann didn't like his son's political passion—it was too dangerous— and remained stubbornly silent.

"All right, I'll tell you. The Jewish cultural community in Vienna has already given large sums to aid Schuschnigg's voting project," Januck said. "Secretly, of course."

Magda kicked Ingria under the table, but Ingria didn't really know why.

Papa wiped the corner of his mouth and said to himself in his usual patient tone, which always calmed Ingria,

"We'll just have to trust the referendum that Schuschnigg has arranged. After all, it's just a few days from now,"

Januck peered solemnly at them.

"He's already requested support from the underground left, and the Jews have donated significant sums of money, like they did before, but," That 'but' made them all hold their breath, even Magda, who seemed to be drinking in every word—these were exciting times for her, as she told Ingria later that evening. But now they were waiting for what came after that ominous 'but'.

"But the Nazis will come, and prevent the vote; that's my guess," Januck continued. "I hope to God I'm wrong." He stared at his empty plate. Margit laid her slender hand over his.

At that moment, Mrs. Waldermann, who had

remained silent throughout this conversation, said somewhat shyly, "Both of the girls are going to be in Sister Elke's drawing class at the arts academy. Isn't that nice?"

"To art," Mama said, and raised her water glass. The glass, however, was empty—a little detail Ingria remembered later, and how Mama tried to get at least a tiny drop to trickle into her mouth. She even tapped the bottom of the glass, to no avail, and murmured, "Good grief." Mrs. Waldermann got up and Mama waved her hand to say there was no need to get her more water and set her glass down like she'd been beaten.

"So, where were we?" she said with her hand around the empty glass, like someone returning from some private excursion.

"A toast to art!" Margit said then, and poured some wine from her own glass into her mother's. "You too, girls!"

And they all clinked their glasses, Mama looked relieved, and Ingria saw a light in Margit's eyes as she looked at Januck and said, "Will you play us something..?"

Januck got up from the table, gave a little bow, and walked to the piano.

"Ladies and gentlemen, honored guests," he said with a playful smile,

"What will it be?"

"Mama likes Chopin,"Margit said.

"But are you sure that's appropriate..?" Papa said, his eyes wandering around the table.

"Particularly the C-sharp minor. Right, Mama?" Margit continued, and Mama's face lit up with a sunny smile. "You and I have always understood each other so well," Mama replied, and Papa's gaze fled to the shadowed corners of the room, then down at the table.

"There is nothing as wonderful as *l'amour*," Mama said, clapping as the piece finished. "In honor of *l'amour*, play *Bei Mir Bist Du Schön*. A duet. Margit, if you please. Januck dear, bitte, bitte schön."

As the music filled the room, Mama put her hand on Papa's knee and whispered, "Their children will surely be musical—and here in Vienna, too. Just think of it, darling—our grandchildren!" and for the first time in a long time, a broad smile spread across Papa's face.

～

Later that afternoon, Mrs. Waldermann returned from shopping breathless and sweaty and the moment she came in the door, even though there was no one in the hall, she said "They're everywhere now."

"Who is, Mrs. Waldermann?" asked Ingria, who happened to be in earshot.

"People with Nazi symbols."

Januck appeared on the upstairs landing, his cheeks a little red, and his mother said, "Januck, the police are wearing swastika armbands."

After dinner they all gathered around the radio to hear a speech by Kurt von Schuschnigg, the chancellor. When he said he was going to cancel the national referendum and resign his post, Januck pounded his chest with his fist and yelled "No. No." so many times that they could hardly hear the chancellor when he said that he had ordered the armed forces to "offer no resistance".

"What about the Jews? What will happen to them?" Mama cried, and Margit hid her tear-stained face in her hands.

"Let's listen," Mr. Waldermann said, turning the radio up. Everyone got quiet, even Januck, and they heard Schuschnigg's final words:

"We have yielded to force. God protect Austria."

~

That night in bed Magda was tossing and turning. She sat up.

"Can't sleep?" Ingria asked.

Magda shook her head and got out of bed.

"Where are you going?"

"To the kitchen. I'm going to get some elderflower juice. Do you want some?"

Ingria nodded and the door swung closed as Magda's shadow disappeared into the hallway.

Tiptoeing down the hall, Magda heard a low murmur of voices from the living room. She stopped and stood behind the heavy velvet curtain to listen.

"It would be wise for you to leave as soon as possible," her father was saying to Ingria's parents.

"But they don't know anything about my grandmother's Jewish ancestry," Ingria's mother said.

"And we don't even practice the religion. I'm sorry to disappoint them, but all that was forgotten in my parents' generation."

"My dear Lilja, they'll consider you a Jew—and your children, too," Magda's father said. "Which means that to stay here would, unfortunately, be dangerous."

"But it never was before," Ingria's mother said with a hint of bitterness in her voice.

"Please don't misunderstand me," Magda's father continued. "It's just that Hitler has an obsessive need to pry into people's genealogy."

"It's pathological," Ingria's father added.

"But we're Nordic people. Finns. He can't do anything to us."

"There's no telling what a person like Hitler will do."

"All right. We'll reserve tickets to Finland as soon as we can. Frankly, I'm beginning to feel quite homesick."

When Magda returned to the bedroom, she didn't bring any juice with her.

The next morning, Magda's side of the bed was empty. Ingria started to get up, and heard rushing footsteps on the stairs.

"Wake up! The German army crossed the border last night!" It was Januck.

HELDENPLATZ

The adults were talking in tense voices about the Anschluss. Januck hadn't come down to breakfast, so Mrs. Waldermann asked the girls to go and get him. Januck told them that the occupation had taken away his appetite.

"Are we going to go listen to the Führer's speech?" Magda asked from the doorway. Her brother was sitting on the bed with his head in his hands.

Januck raised his eyes. "*The Führer?*"

There were sounds in the hallway and Mr. Waldermann appeared in the door behind Ingria and Magda. He said that Hitler was giving a speech on the Heldenplatz, from the balcony of Hofburg Palace. Mama hurried up and stood beside him, her face red and splotchy.

"I want to see that crook with my own eyes before I leave Vienna," she said.

Papa's voice rang out from downstairs: "Lilja, I don't think that's wise."

"Who else wants to go?" Mr. Waldermann asked, peering at each of them.

"I do," Magda said.

Ingria wasn't surprised. Magda'd had her nose pressed against the window all afternoon, watching as their formerly quiet street was flooded with ecstatic-looking crowds carrying swastika flags.

~

Papa was right, Ingria thought. They shouldn't have come to Heldenplatz. The crowd was so large that it frightened her, and she held tightly to Papa's hand to keep from being swept away by the flood of people. From someplace far away, Hitler's voice rumbled like a roll of thunder: "Als Führer und Kanzler der deutschen Nation und des Reiches melde ich vor der deutschen Geschichte nunmehr den Eintritt meiner Heimat in das Deutsche Reich."

Then Mama put her mouth to Papa's ear and said, in whispered Finnish, that with just one sentence Austria had been lost. A lady glared at them angrily, and Papa didn't answer.

After a moment, he said in German, "Let's stand right here," and they stopped at a street corner. They wouldn't have been able to get closer anyway because the whole area was thick with people and fluttering swastika flags, and somewhere beyond all the heads and broad shoulders the voice of Hitler blared. The crowd bobbed around Ingria like a restless sea, and every so often they shouted "One people, one reich, one leader!"

Magda whispered to her father and he lifted her above the crowd for a moment. Ingria saw how her eyes were glittering and dark with excitement. Magda waved to Ingria, telling her she should look too, and Ingria's papa lifted her up for a moment. She saw the tiny, faraway figure that was the source of the deafening voice. Then a man shoved Papa and shouted, Put the girl down! and Papa immediately obeyed. Ingria held onto her father, dizzy, as if she'd just climbed down from her seat on the ferris wheel at Prater and couldn't find her footing.

When Hitler finally finished speaking, Mama said that it was offensive to hold such an event in front of a castle of the Habsburgs. Then Papa whispered, "Lilja, please." But Mama wanted the people around them to hear what she had to say. "What a display! And in this of all places. But what can you expect from such a barbarian?"

Ingria noticed that a grim-looking man standing nearby was staring hard at Mama. Then the man suddenly stretched out his hand and introduced himself, and Mama told him her own name, and said, "Nice to meet you." Januck grabbed hold of Mama's arm and said "We should be leaving," and he seemed to hustle her away into the crowd. Mama turned to the grim man and shouted, "Auf Wiedersehen."

As they approached the Waldermann's house Ingria turned to look behind them, as if the strange man's icy stare might be following her, and she jumped with fright when she saw someone disappear around the corner near the bakery. But it was probably nothing, just her own fear.

"Now I'll have quite a story to tell when we get home," Mama said, but everyone else walked in silence.

"There were some happy people there too, though," Magda said suddenly. Ingria noticed the sharp look Januck gave his sister.

"Only philistines greet another philistine with joy," Mama said.

Magda stiffened, but Ingria was the only one who noticed.

THE STRANGER

One afternoon, Margit spent some time helping Ingria with her mathematics so she wouldn't fall behind in her studies. After the lesson, Ingria went to the window to watch for Magda coming home from school. Then she saw someone she recognized: the man from Heldenplatz, the one with the icy stare, walking down their street just below her. He disappeared around a corner, but Ingria could see that he had stopped walking. The sun still cast his strange, elongated shadow over the sidewalk. She waited for the shadow to continue on its way, but it didn't move. Magda appeared and was about to walk past the long, unnatural shadow, but she stopped and went back to where the man was standing and they formed one misshapen shadow, like a creature with long arms and short arms, long legs and short legs, and two heads. A monster. Ingria was trembling. But she had to watch the shadow play to the end. The arms waved, then the short, plump shadow raised one arm up at an angle, straight and stiff. What were they talking about for such a long time, and who was that man?

Ingria carefully opened the window a crack. She heard a murmur but couldn't hear any words, until suddenly the word "Pflicht" came to her, as if carried on the wind. Duty. That's what it meant. Maybe he was talking about going to school? The shadow monster split in two, and Magda came running to the front door with a broad smile on her face.

That evening Magda said they should play Third Reich Princess, and she reached in her pocket and pulled out a handful of sweets wrapped in gold paper. Inside each candy was a ring with a swastika carved in it.

A PORTRAIT OF HITLER

Sister Elke taught drawing class twice a week on the ground floor of the Vienna Academy of Fine Arts, in room number 5. Papa was taking them to class, because the city was restless and Januck hadn't yet come back from the university.

On the tram, Ingria sat next to Papa and Magda sat in the seat in front of them.

As the tram turned onto Opernring they saw some women and men bent over the sidewalk, washing it with scrub brushes. Around them stood a laughing crowd of men in Nazi insignia and ordinary passersby. Ingria looked at Papa, but he was staring straight ahead, his face frozen. She craned to see out the window. On the sidewalk was written "Vote for Schuschnigg". The scrubbing had already removed some of the letters. The hard eyes of the people on the street frightened

Ingria, and she pressed herself up against Papa, and he looked at her. His eyes were shattered with sorrow.

Then Magda spun around in her seat and said, "Jews. They supported Chancellor Schuschnigg, remember?"

Ingria looked at Magda, the disdainful curve of her lips, but she didn't answer because Papa was squeezing her hand. It felt like he wanted her to be quiet.

As they got off the tram, Ingria held Papa's hand and Magda played hopscotch on the sidewalk ahead of them. Ingria slowed her steps. "Papa, I don't want to go to drawing class. Can't I stay home today?"

"Ingria, the Waldermanns have been very kind to us, and it would be impolite to refuse to go to your drawing lesson. My evening star isn't going to misbehave, is she?" Then he suddenly looked around, as if he was afraid of something. There was no one there. Much later, Ingria remembered this, the uneasy look in his eyes, but at that moment she was comforted by her old nickname. He hadn't used it in a long time.

When they got to the school, she looked at her father again. He seemed to have suddenly grown older in some inexplicable way, like something had turned him to stone, turned him into a mountain like the ones she'd seen in the Waldermanns' foreign magazines. A mountain covered in ash. That picture had made her sad, as if life itself were buried. She had thought about the flowers and the animals covered over and smothered by the lava.

Magda was holding the door open, waiting. Watching them.

"Papa, don't leave me here."

Ingria didn't know herself why she said this. Maybe it was the fear she sensed all around her, in the streets and the cafes, the fear that had finally walked through the door into the Waldermanns' house, too, and taken hold of her.

"Everything will be all right," Papa said. She noticed a few drops of sweat along his hairline.

"Ingria," he said, gently stroking her cheek, "You can always count on Sister Elke to help you. Go along now."

Ingria let go of his hand and ran up the steps to the school door. When she turned back to look, Papa was already walking away, his head bent, his hands clasped behind his back. "Papa!" she shouted. He turned and smiled at her. Then Magda tugged her arm in irritation, pulling her inside.

The figure of Sister Elke, moving among the rows of drawing tables, draped in her long black habit, inspired an instinctive respect in Ingria, although she didn't really understand why some people turned away from worldly life. Maybe Sister Elke really was above all earthly desire, like Magda said she was.

Ingria peeked over her sketchpad at Sister Elke, who had small, shining eyes and a large, cracked mole on her cheek. Ingria thought she must be older than Mama, but not as old as their housekeeper Emma. Emma had gray hair.

Sister Elke's drawing class usually passed in silent concentration once she had given them their assignment and a brief lesson—as she had today about adding lights and shadows to a composition.

Ingria bent over her work. Every now and then Sister Elke would look up from the pile of papers in front of her and let her gaze wander over her diligent pupils. Sometimes she would get up and walk among them, not saying much except to perhaps give a word of encouragement if a little hand paused hesitantly. Now she was standing next to Ingria's seat.

"Excellent."

Ingria glanced at Magda, who smiled. Ingria smiled back.

In the middle of this leisurely lesson there was a knock at the door. Before Sister Elke could answer, the door swung open and a squat, red-faced man strode in. Ingria remembered seeing the man the day Papa brought a sample of her drawings to the school.

"Say good day to Rector Bauer, girls," Sister Elke said. They stood and greeted him in unison:

"Good day, Rector Bauer."

"Good day," he answered. "I have a commission for you." He whispered something to Sister Elke and placed a stack of photographs on her desk. Sister Elke's face hardened.

"Do your best, girls," the rector said. "Your portraits will be entered in a competition." Then he hurried out the door.

Sister Elke asked the class to put their still lifes away in the cabinet and handed each pupil a photo from the pile. When Ingria's turn came, she gave a start:

Hitler. His eyes stared at her like two cinders. Not burnt cinders. Flaming. What was the fire burning him, Ingria wondered as she went back to her seat. She looked at the picture for a long time. She remembered the voice thundering over the heads of the crowd—a voice with a passion that filled her with fear, and filled others with ecstasy. His mouth. It was a weak, almost puny mouth. But it had a voice that could move national boundaries. Ingria picked up her chalk.

For the next three hours the pupils labored with their heads bent over their portraits, and just as the hour was about to end, Rector Bauer tapped on the door and came into the room. Sister Elke stiffly asked the class to write their names on their drawings and carry them up to the front. On a whim, Ingria wrote along the bottom, in letters so unobtrusive that it was hard to make them out, the name Amalie Rhein.

Rector Bauer looked at each drawing appraisingly and placed them in two piles as Sister Elke looked on in silence. Magda's drawing went in the pile on the left. Magda's face shone with triumph: hers had been picked. When Rector Bauer came to Ingria's drawing, he smiled for the first time. "Quite good," he said, and put it in the pile on the right.

Ingria cast her eyes down, hoping she wouldn't be discovered, but she could sense Magda looking at her. As each drawing was sorted, Ingria heard sighs and quiet sniffs around her. She heard them every time the rector's hand placed a drawing in one of the piles. Ingria didn't dare look around the room.

Finally the rector left, taking the pictures he'd chosen, and Sister Elke put the rest in the cabinet.

"The winner will be announced later, when all the talented children in Vienna have had a chance to participate," she said drily, and strode out of the classroom.

Magda and Ingria stood in front of the school waiting for Januck, who had promised to pick them up when he was finished at the university. Magda didn't speak to Ingria, just played hopscotch on the sidewalk. When six o'clock came and the streets began to grow dark, Magda stopped and said that they'd better walk home. Ingria was frightened. "If Januck can't come, Papa will come to get us," she said. Then Magda turned to look at her.

"Come on, or I'll leave you here."

As they walked—it felt to Ingria like an eternity— the streets dimmed to black and the milk-glass eyes of the street lamps were frightening, watchful, just as if they were arching their long necks to peer down at the two girls below them.

"How much farther?" Ingria asked.

"Not much farther. We're almost home," Magda said in a bored tone, but Ingria could tell she felt uneasy, and when she took hold of Magda's hand, Magda didn't pull away. Maybe Magda had thawed toward her, put the drawing competition out of her mind.

After a moment of silence, Magda said, "That's where Hadar used to live."

The house looked deserted. Sad, with its long, dark windows.

"Where'd they go?" Ingria asked.

"Hadar said they were moving to Canada."

They walked some more in silence, each listening to her own footsteps.

The windows of the Waldermanns' stone house came into view, and they too were dark.

"Nobody's home," Ingria whispered and squeezed Magda's hand tighter. "That's why no one came."

~

Over the following days and nights they waited hour after hour for the slam of the door, the merry murmur of voices drifting from the foyer, for everything to go back to the way it was, as if this silence was just a mistake, a room they had to walk through. But no one came.

The apartment felt frozen, motionless. Ingria sat on the living-room sofa, slowly swinging her feet. Magda had gone into the bedroom. There was no sound from her.

Ingria got up and went to her parents' bedroom. She stepped over the threshold and stood staring at the hairbrush on the dresser. A few of her mother's hairs poked out of it. She looked at the little oval dish where her mother put her hairpins when she loosened her chignon. The lipstick. Mama hadn't gone far away, because it was still there on the dresser.

It felt as if the whole house had died. There was

no one talking, no one looking at her, no clatter of silverware, no shouts or laughter. None of the life that she used to sense with every breath, even through the walls.

She felt cold.

Then she heard a rustle, turned and caught a glimpse of Magda's gray flannel dress, the hem fluttering as she disappeared into the long, dark hallway. Suddenly, Ingria was struck by a rush of rage at Januck. Why had he lured Margit here to marry him? Sent all those letters and made the whole family come to this country, where she was all alone now? Where was everyone? Why didn't they come back? Why did they leave her here?

Her cheeks burned with the mute rage that had been hiding inside her as the days passed. She wished she could run right through the walls of the building, run right through the whole world, to Vyborg, to her Emma's arms, to bury her head in Emma's blue checked apron and tell her she'd had a bad dream.

～

At night Ingria and Magda slept pressed against each other, their tears and hopelessness falling onto the same pillow. They heard neighbors' doors slamming, running steps, chilling shouts that made them stay inside, eating dry bits of bread from the pantry with crystalized honey Mama had brought from home and some forgotten crusts of zwieback they found in the back of the cupboard.

They went from window to window, not daring to open the curtains, watching from between the heavy drapes as men in almond-colored uniforms marched through the streets and shoved people into trucks with the butts of their rifles. Ingria looked at Magda, who had her mother's amethysts dangling from her ears. "Can you call your relatives?" Ingria asked. Magda didn't know their telephone number. "Then let's go to their house," Ingria said. "To Hungary, you mean?" Magda said and rolled her eyes.

By the third day, when they had eaten the last dregs of honey from the bottom of the jar, Magda suddenly said, "This is your fault. You're foreigners. And foreigners always spoil things." A little later she said, "Hitler doesn't like foreigners." Ingria didn't know what to say to that. Magda shoved the jar at her and disappeared somewhere into the house.

Ingria didn't say another word to her for the rest of the day but when night came Magda wrapped an arm around her and she could feel her own heartbeat throbbing in her temple. She didn't know anyone in this big city; she was a foreigner. Then she remembered what Papa said before they parted. You can always trust Sister Elke to help you.

The next morning Ingria asked, "should we go to drawing class?" Magda thought for a moment, and said, "Alright."

As they walked out onto the street, Magda looked at the swastika flags hanging from the houses fluttering in the wind.

"Isn't it nice though? It's like there's a festival every day."

"Yes,' Ingria said, because she remembered that the houses had ears.

As she walked beside Magda into the arts academy, it felt as if the whole massive building was holding its breath, just listening for their echoing step. There was only a faint hint of the smell of paint in the high-ceilinged corridor, a hint of their vanished life.

Magda knocked on the teachers' office door, and when Sister Elke appeared with questioning eyes, told her that they had been left alone and they had no idea where their parents were. All expression froze on Sister Elke's face, as if she had been wrenched from a peaceful dream and thrust into broad daylight. She made an immediate decision that they should return to the Waldermanns' house, and pulled her thick black coat off its hanger.

On the sidewalk, Ingria held tight to Sister Elke's hand. The city had turned threatening. There were armed soldiers on the street corners. Ingria kept her head down, but she couldn't help noticing a soldier painting the familiar window of Café Rembrandt with big white letters that said 'Jew'.

"Only enough food and supplies for three days!" A man's voice roared from inside as they approached. Men, women and children with suitcases were rushed out the door into the back of a truck. They had yellow stars on their lapels.

"Hurry up! Faster!" The soldier shouted, striking

a woman in the back with his rifle butt. The woman fell, but then gathered herself up and stood again.

Ingria glanced at Sister Elke who seemed frozen. Ingria didn't dare ask her where the people were being taken.

Stuffy air greeted them as they stepped into the shadowy hallway of the Waldermanns' house.

"Put your clothes on the bed, girls," Sister Elke said "Be quick." Something in the tone of her voice lent an unpleasant tinge to the half-darkened bedroom. Then she went out into the hallway. They heard doors open and close, open and close. What's she looking for? Ingria wondered, continuing to pile clothes on the bed. It was a modest pile. Long pink bloomers, undershirts, socks, sweaters, flannel dresses, blouses. Magda dashed back and forth between the wardrobe and the closet, heaping all her clothes in a great mound on the bed.

"We'll leave quite soon," Sister Elke said from the doorway. She had a large suitcase in each hand. One of them belonged to Mama and Papa.

Sister Elke quickly sorted through Ingria's clothing. "You won't need this at the convent." It was the pale blue silk dress made especially for her, for Margit's wedding. Ingria didn't dare argue. "Right. You can put the rest of these in your suitcase," Sister Elke said, and circled to the other side of the bed.

Magda's cheeks reddened as Sister Elke picked up party dresses from per pile and set them aside. "No... no..." she said again and again. To a pair of black Mary Janes, " No."

"These are new shoes, Sister Elke," Magda said, her eyes moist as she swallowed back tears.

"You need sturdier shoes than that," Sister Elke said calmly. "Let's see if we can find some more useful things. Come along."

There was nothing in Ingria's parents' room but Mama's high heels and Papa's patent leather shoes.

"Wait here, girls." Sister Elke went out again.

"I'm going to look like quite a hick in these old sweaters," Magda said. She picked up Ingria's mother's lipstick from the bureau.

"Give that to me," said Ingria, stretching her hand out. There was arrogance in Magda's eyes as she slipped the lipstick into her pocket.

"That belongs to my mother," Ingria said, but she fell silent when Sister Elke returned carrying a pair of worn gray-green leather ankle boots.

"Those are Januck's old walking shoes, Sister." Sister Elke shoved them into a suitcase.

ON A JOURNEY SOMEWHERE

Januck couldn't bear to watch his wife's parents asleep on the floor of the train car. He turned away, and smelled Margit's faintly sour breath. After the interrogation they'd been ordered onto the train with the other prisoners. Januck had lost his sense of time and ruminated about where they were being taken.

He straightened his back warily so he wouldn't wake Margit and slowly put his arm around her shoulder. He heard the door open. Someone was doing their business. The stink of diarrhea wafted through the air and intermingled with the dense smell of sweat and vomit. They crowded around the boarded-up windows but no fresh air could get through. They just had to wait.

Januck looked at the men and women around him, their pale sleeping faces. How peaceful they looked when they were asleep, almost like children, innocent. The fear fled their faces, and the faces of his wife's parents rocking on the floor to the rhythm of the train. They looked so different now, as if the life was already starting to drain away from them as the torturous, uncertain days passed.

The shock in their eyes when the men came to take them away. His father asleep in his chair, awakened when the barrel of a gun was shoved into his chest. The cold eyes of the men in their uniforms as they swept through the room. Margit with a glass of juice in her hand, standing in the kitchen doorway, Januck and his father-in-law Unto reading the newspaper. Lilja on the plush sofa, absorbed in a book about Mahler. His mother, her face red as she came out of the kitchen with a towel in her hand. "This is some sort of misunderstanding," Lilja said at the front door, seeming so certain as she threw her best flowered scarf over her shoulder, the one with purple flowers.

That scarf hung dirty and torn from her neck now, its brilliant flowers vaguely faded. Everything else was taken from her. They made her take it all off and leave it on the table—the earrings, the necklace, everything. Even her wedding ring. Just the thought of Lilja's naked female body before those cold eyes made Januck twitch with shame, though his medical studies had make him familiar with the human body. Just then, Lilja opened her eyes, as if reading his thoughts, and said through colorless lips, "La bête humaine," then closed them again.

Januck held Margit tighter in his arms.

He felt the train car suddenly tilt. They seemed to be turning a corner.

"A member of the resistance." Margit's parents' eyes had frozen when they heard that. Unto's eyebrows went up, his blue eyes stared at Januck as if seeing him for the first time. A gaze that said, Just who are you exactly? That had been almost as bad as the blows in the interrogation.

"They don't know anything," Januck said again and again between blows. "Let them go, for god's sake," he pleaded. None of them had dared to mention the two little girls waiting at home, so they wouldn't be picked up too, taken somewhere they might never return from.

His stepmother silently wept and Lilja's face was grey and frozen. Margit. Margit was the only one who knew about his political activities. "You're doing the right thing," she had said once, with a special brightness in her eyes. At the time, seeing her bravery had made his love feel stronger than before, almost a physical pain. The train slowed and came to a stop.

Januck took hold of Margit's slender hand. Her eyes began to open.

Where were they?

Through the boarded windows, Januck saw only the black boots of soldiers marching back and forth.

When they were ordered off the train no one said anything. They were a shivering mass, numb with cold and hunger. Margit pressed fearfully against him, but a soldier tore her away and ordered women, children and old people to the left, working-aged men to the right.

Januck looked at Margit, his eyes drowning in hers, then went with the other men through the wide, guarded gate.

AMALIE RHEIN

Rector Bauer stood in his office at the Vienna Academy of Fine Arts and stared out the window at Schiller Park. He had just received the results of the children's drawing contest, and the winning drawings lay in his hand. How ironic that a man who had twice tried to get into the academy had now been made the subject of the drawing contest. It was positively grotesque. And what would Hitler's cultural politics lead to? No art but German Nationalist art? The art of Nazi idealism? Destruction. It would lead to inevitable destruction. Bauer snapped back to reality and found himself staring at the back of the statue of Schiller. He glanced at the drawing in his hand. There was no question that it was an excellent drawing, with an unusually sensitive line.

He had to do this. The artist was to receive a prize at a Nazi ceremony. The planning had already begun.

Bauer looked around for the lists of pupils. Where had he put them? Before she had been transported to a labor camp, his secretary Ruth had written out neat name tags for all the folders and notebooks. "So you'll be able to find everything easily while I'm gone," she'd said.

But he couldn't find a pupil named Amalie Rhein on any of the lists. Sweat beaded on his brow.

"Wait a minute," Bauer muttered, remembering a foreign man who had left his daughter's drawings for Sister Elke. Bauer had only glanced at them quickly, but he thought they might have had that same quality of line.

He found the drawings in the cabinet and took them out of their folder. A little smile of relief flickered across his face. Yes, it was the same artist. The name on the drawings was Ingria Silo. And the address was Mr. and Mrs. Waldermann's.

~

An hour later Bauer walked down the peaceful street to the house but the name on the door was not Waldermann but Ruff. He stood in front of the door, uncertain. Just then, a window opened. A boy about 10 years old aimed a toy pistol at him. "What do you want?" the boy said with a fierce look. "Sorry, wrong house," Bauer said, and hurried away. Behind him he heard the boy imitate the sound of pistol shots. Bam! Bam, bam!

When he was a few blocks away, Bauer opened

the top button of his coat and loosened his necktie. The pastry shop caught his eye.

As he stepped into the warm aroma of wheat, a pimple-faced shop assistant came out of the back room. The boy peered at him questioningly. Bauer ordered two eszterhazys and as he paid he asked in as natural a voice as he could if the Waldermanns and their guests had gone abroad.

"They were picked up. The whole lot of them," the boy said.

"The children too?"

"A nun came and got the girls. Magda and the other one. There's a new family living there now."

"How long ago was that?" Bauer ventured to ask, since the boy seemed to be a blabbermouth. But a suspicious look suddenly flashed in the boy's eyes.

"I'll ask the baker," he said. Bauer told him it wasn't important, and hurried out the door.

Bauer felt a sense of relief as his car passed through the green landscape, leaving the city behind. Vienna had been transformed overnight. His lively city was now just a pale memory of its former self, like a frozen picture on a postcard. From its balconies flooded crude, tasteless flags announcing the occupation. And he was supposed to give a speech about the man who made it all happen. How could he mention in his speech the fact that Hitler as a young man had dreamed of a career as an artist and even tried to get into the Vienna Academy of Fine Arts, more than once, and been rejected? He could never mention that in his younger days Hitler had sat in Vienna's street cafés painting bland watercolor cityscapes with weak perspective. Periods of civility are always followed by barbarism—didn't Schopenhauer say that?

Bauer drove past an idyllic village and turned onto a small side road just beyond a granary. The gray convent peeped out from between the trees. He hoped to find the girl there.

Magda had finished sweeping the stone floor of the corridor—a chore she hated—and was on her way to clean the broom when she saw a short, plump man she recognized coming toward her—Rector Bauer. Ingria must have made it into the final competition! Or maybe even won the prize. Why else would the Rector of the academy be there? Where was Ingria? Probably wandering in the woods. Magda was overcome by a fierce surge of anticipation and curiosity. It led her to the door that Rector Bauer had just closed behind him.

Bauer looked around the stark room, the whitewashed walls, the simple wooden furniture waxed and polished to a shine, the window looking out on a patch of glowing green landscape. He sat down in the chair Sister Elke offered him. When he finished the glass of delicious elderflower juice she gave him, he told her about the Nazi gala. It was to celebrate the importance of National Socialist art and Hitler's grand project to amass a world-class collection of art for a planned museum in Linz.

"The museum will include Hitler's art as well," Bauer added, his face red.

Sister Elke gave him a meaningful look.

"Anyway, the winner of the children's drawing contest is going to be announced at the gala." Bauer wiped the sweat from his brow. This was what his work had come to.

"The girl can't leave the convent," Sister Elke said, her hands folded sedately in her lap. "She's under our protection."

"But the girl has to be there," Rector Bauer said, and paused."And she has to be a German girl."

Bauer pondered how he would explain to the audience that Mr. and Mrs. Rhein, the parents of the winner of the drawing contest, hadn't honored the ceremony with their presence. But first he had to get this stubborn nun to agree to the whole ridiculous project.

"Neither one of us wants any trouble," Bauer said.

Just then Sister Elke tilted her head. Something had cast a shadow under the door. A very unpleasant feeling washed over Bauer. He looked uncertainly at Sister Elke, and she swiftly stood up and pulled the door open. Bauer craned to look but he couldn't see who was in the doorway. He heard running footsteps.

"Magda! Come back here this minute!" Sister Elke said in a hard, sharp voice that echoed down the corridor.

"I'm sorry sister," a girl's voice said faintly.

"You will perform two weeks' penance in the cellar chamber. Go to your room and wait for me there."

Bauer craned his neck again, caught a glimpse of

the girl's teary eyes, and pitied her. But after all God's work was none of his business.

The following week a gleaming black car pulled up in front of the convent, where Ingria stood waiting beside Sister Elke. She could feel the slapdash bow Sister Elke had put in her hair flattened beneath her hat like a swatted butterfly. The sisters had also sewed her a black dress with a white collar.

As she walked to the car, Ingria glanced at the cellar window and saw Magda watching her through the grating. It crushed her soul. But there was nothing she could do but get in the car that would take her to the arts academy.

~

Ingria gazed with curiosity through the car window at the streets of Vienna. It felt as if the city had fallen into an unfathomable dejection. As they neared the arts academy they passed the Burgkino cinema. On the sign, in large letters, was: *Der Fall Deruga*. Ingria wondered what kind of movie that was.

As the car pulled up in front of the academy, Ingria was overcome with uneasiness. Men in uniforms and women in fancy dresses crowded the entrance, chattering happily. How was she going to survive this evening? What if they discovered that she had written a false name on her drawing? And that she was a foreigner? Then Rector Bauer appeared at the door and smiled encouragingly.

~

Mr. Bauer stood behind the curtain and scanned his speech nervously. Writing it had been the most humiliating experience of his life. But he had to do it.

When the audience grew quiet he stepped onto the brightly lit stage, gazed out at the staring crowd, and said a few polite words about the important role the Vienna Academy of Fine Arts had once played when they had, without knowing it, relinquished Adolf Hitler to the much greater task that lay before him. The audience exploded into a storm of applause and Bauer thought, God, what idiots. He continued with flowery words about the rise of National Socialist art and its significance and felt the red shame spread over his face.

~

"When is it my turn?" Ingria asked Sister Elke, who was standing beside her backstage. Sister Elke whispered, "Patience." When she heard Rector Bauer invite Amalie Rhein, the winner of the drawing contest, onto the stage, she couldn't move. No. That's not me, a voice in her head pounded. But Sister Elke bent toward her and whispered, "Go on. Quickly."

As she walked into the spotlight, Ingria felt the sharp edge of the bow in her hair scrape her temple, her stiff petticoat rustling with every trembling step. There was a sudden silence as she reached out her hand to take the bouquet of flowers and the gold-embossed certificate from Rector Bauer. She saw his frozen eyes, the thin vein pulsing at his temple.

"Danke schön," she said softly and gave a deep curtsy. She hardly dared to look at the clapping crowd, sparkling with women in evening gowns, high ranking Nazi officers in their medals, and staring faces filled with festive solemnity.

"Bring out the parents!" Someone in the crowd shouted.

Rector Bauer's face turned serious, and the audience went quiet.

"Honored guests, it falls on me to tell you that this little girl just awarded a prize is one of our nation's many orphans of war."

The crowd burst into furious applause. Ingria curtsied again and walked as if drugged back to Sister Elke, who stood waiting between two stony-faced soldiers. Then Ingria remembered Hadar, the girl whose parents had taken her out of the country. All the way to Canada. How lucky she was.

The music started and Rector Bauer returned to them. "Well, that went well," he said.

"I want to go home," Ingria said in a barely audible whisper, gazing into Bauer's dimmed eyes. Something in that fierce gaze made the rector uncomfortable.

"My father told me that art would rescue me," the girl added suddenly, her eyes still locked on his.

"You must always trust in that," he said as convincingly as he could, and watched as she and Sister Elke disappeared through the door.

THE THIRD AUTUMN AT
THE CONVENT

Ingria woke in the early morning and saw that Magda's bed was empty. She got dressed and went outside. Sometimes she took her sketchpad and pastels with her, but usually she just walked around the convent grounds, and sometimes to the nearby village, just beyond the field and granary.

Autumn would soon be over, Ingria thought, looking around at the empty fields where they had spent the long days, and she missed their time walking in the forest in a large group gathering up what the land had to offer: wild blackberries, mushrooms, herbs, sometimes even roots, twigs, and evergreen cones.

As she walked along the edge of the woods she noticed sparkling crystal frost in the muddy furrows of a potato field, like a reminder that winter was on its way, but wasn't yet ready to make its attack on nature, was merely giving a promise of storms, snow, and ice. The soil was still moist and warm, resisting as if it had its own will, the will of the earth, expressed in the light breath of mist that wafted from the ground into the air.

Ingria sat down on a rotted stump blossoming with moss. How she loved these morning moments, when nature felt like the only thing whose persevering existence no one could change. When she could go on a journey in her mind. She often returned home. Went back to the pond to watch the silly, staring little fish with their mouths open, the snowflakes melting on Papa's coat collar, Mama at the dinner table, smiling, without a hint of headache. Emma's mouth stretched wide like a rubber band as she sat chattering in the kitchen or bustled over a big pot, the pink foam rising to the surface of the lingonberries, the steam dimming the windows. Everything else she left out, as if the sketchpad of her mind had blank pages she didn't know how to fill, white pages where she couldn't draw a single line or form a single shape.

She looked around. The trees and bushes calmed her, reminded her how soon they would shake off their leaves, form buds when winter was over, each bud unfurling into a glowing green leaf she could take in her hand. Like a flower that comes up every spring, brave and indifferent to everything. And she waited. She waited for the change, as certain of it as nature around her was certain of itself.

But uncertainty still gnawed at her. She filled her lungs with fresh morning air, its steady peace.

The abbess had told her that as long as she was at the convent she was safe.

As she walked back Ingria wondered if Magda had met someone. Lately she'd been sneaking off to the village, simply climbed out the window after the nuns had fallen asleep.

Last Thursday, as Magda was on her way out, Ingria noticed that her lips were painted a deep magenta.

"You have Mama's lipstick," Ingria said.

"So what?" Magda answered, climbing up on a chair.

"Give it to me. It belongs to me!" She could hear the trembling squeak in her voice as she grabbed the hem of Magda's coat.

"Let go of me, you kike!"

And she let go, startled at what Magda had said. What did she mean?

Once Magda had wriggled through the narrow window, she looked for Mama's lipstick in the candlelight, searched everywhere. It belonged to her. It was all she had left. But she couldn't find it. When Magda returned in the middle of the night she smelled of pungent life, tobacco, beer. She was 16 and voluptuous, and with Mama's dark lipstick she looked like a woman. Ingria was certain she'd been at the village tavern. What did she tell them about herself there? She didn't tell them what had happened in Vienna, that was certain.

ANOTHER TIME, ANOTHER TRAIN

Januck dozed with the other bald, hollow-cheeked men in the cattle car. The torture of lice was over. They had been shaved before the transfer, all the way to the genitals, left scraped and bloody. You can be grateful for so little when it's a lot. A torment that made sleeping impossible, verged on madness. But the memory of it was visible on his scalp. It was covered in the scars of louse bites.

As the train rocked, Januck tried to sleep, but sleep wouldn't come, only wavering images. Most of all Margit's face. It flickered like sun and shadow on a beautiful summer day. Margit smiling, a ray of light refracted in her golden brown eyes. Eyes like drops of amber. Januck smiled back. Margit pale, sleeping nestled against his shoulder. Her lips slightly open.

Unto and Lilja on the floor, leaning against each other, their faces shaking with the rumble of the train. Januck stirred restlessly and opened his eyes. Where were they? Margit? Her parents? It took him a moment to remember that this was a different time, a different train. He was in a striped prison uniform now, with other men, traveling to an unknown place. The Mauthausen concentration camp was behind them. Januck's thoughts paused for a moment on a man he knew there. He hoped that the fellow would survive slave labor. That they would meet again someday, under different circumstances, as they'd said they would. His name was Simon Wiesenthal. He was a Jew, and Januck feared the worst.

The train slowed. He could feel it's dreary rhythm in every joint, his body numbed, estranged, a blank cavity. He slowly opened his eyes. He heard the slam of a train car door and noticed that the train had stopped. The guards were making their rounds. For one bright second he saw long grass through the floorboards licked by flashlight beams, and the next second darkness. Januck's feet obeyed before he could think. He stood up and clambered over the other sleeping prisoners. When the guards had moved on, he wrenched open the door and jumped out. He rolled down the embankment into the grass, and no one saw him go. From the wooded darkness he watched the train start into motion and realized that he had escaped.

The long line of cars pulled away and disappeared beyond the edge of the forest, and it took Januck a moment to realize that he was staring at something that was blacker than the night around him. A short distance away stood a freight car on a sidetrack, still and silent. Unable to move, Januck stared at it as if it were a phantom manifested by the night. Why had it been left out in the woods?

He looked around. There were no buildings to be seen. Just forest.

He slowly walked toward it, stood beside it. The bolts were too strong to break without tools.

Then the dark of the sky was broken as the moon revealed itself. Januck stopped and looked up. Gray veils of cloud drifted over the moon, warily shedding their light as if afraid of dissolving.

Januck climbed onto the roof of the car. There was no ventilation grate, but there was a hatch and it wasn't locked, just bolted. There must not be anything valuable inside. The Nazis wouldn't leave anything for thieves to find.

He slid the heavy wrought-iron bolt open and lifted the hatch. A powerful, putrid smell flew up in his face and he instinctively drew back. Then he looked down. Children's faces, made almost translucent by the reflected moonlight. Children with their limbs intertwined. Two-year-olds, twelve-year-olds, lying side by side on the freightcar floor. Holy God, where are you? Girls and boys. Without oxygen, food or water. He saw a braid with a red bow, chubby little hands.

He knew that there was nothing he could do. That there hadn't been for weeks.

THE BLIND SINGER

Ingria watched Magda sleep, her quivering eyelids. What did she dream about? The boys in the village that she met in secret? Who in the world was she? Ingria dressed silently and tiptoed out of the room.

Rambling in the soft, dim morning, her ears came alert. She thought she heard someone singing. She stood still. A thin twig rustled softly under her foot, startling a bird into flight. Where was the song coming from? A thin, beautiful voice like a silver flute. She walked cautiously toward it. Ingria jumped over a ditch and hurried forward with light steps, like Hiawatha in a book she had at home Finland. Who could be singing? It wasn't yet 6 o'clock. Ingria knew that the closest village was at least half an hour's walk away. The voice was heavenly. And she recognized the melody. It was Schubert. *Der Lindenbaum*, a song about the tree of death. She'd heard it with her parents at a concert in Vyborg.

The sound seemed quite close now, and she could see a neglected cottage. There was a woman in the yard, among the tufts of grass and sorrel, singing with her mouth wide open and her eyes shut. It felt as if the forest had gone quiet to listen to her. When the song ended, the woman put her head in her hands and burst into tears, as if her body was buffeted by an anguished wind. Ingria wanted to run away, away from the shame of the song, hidden in the depths of the forest. But she stood and watched until the woman staggered to the house. Then the woman fumbled for the door, and Ingria realized she was blind.

She saw a dark brown bottle in a basket next to the cottage door. It was the same kind of bottle the nuns used for their herbal medicines. Maybe the blind singer was under their protection too. Dangerous in her own way.

For her own part, Ingria felt as if a husk had grown around her, constructing itself bit by bit, until she eventually would disappear from view. But she breathed beneath that husk, for herself, for life.

A VOICE IN THE NIGHT

Januck had been walking along the tracks most of the night when he came to a cluster of farm houses. He approached them warily, behind a screen of trees. He had to get some civilian clothes. Nearing one sturdy, moonlit house, he decided to investigate a shed in the back yard. He circled behind the house, waited a moment, and crept along the wall. If he was lucky he might find a work coat or coveralls.

Januck opened the door. He could hear his own breath as he reached out for some clothing that were hanging from a nail. He quickly swept the clothes over his arm and slipped into the night.

Later, as he spread them out in the moonlight, he saw that he'd got a sweater and trousers, and a lambskin coat, too, though they were for a much stouter man. Januck was almost skin and bone—but the belt would keep the trousers up. He wadded his prison clothes into a roll; they might make do as a pillow. Then he turned his steps back toward the train tracks and set off, hoping to find the girls at the convent outside Vienna.

~

How long had he been walking? He didn't know. The nights and days melted into one long succession of light and darkness.

He ate when he found food, stripping frost-bitten rowan berries from the trees into his mouth and stealing eggs from under sleepy chickens. He ate the eggshells too, for the calcium. If he was lucky he got a drop of stolen milk. But he had to beware of dogs. There seemed to be dogs at every farm, watching from the bushes, their night eyes gleaming.

Before approaching a house, he threw pine cones into the yard, waited, waited, like a hungry wolf lying silently in wait for his prey.

~

After a trek of many weeks, Januck saw the gray convent on a hillside, peeping through the leafy trees. The sight sent a thrill through him. He felt his childhood stirring close by, the innocent summers, the hiking trips there with his family. It filled him with peace. He was almost sure the girls would be there under the nuns' protection. And there would be a place for him there, too, because he knew that as long as Hitler wanted churchgoers to support his politics—or close their eyes to them—he wouldn't touch the convents.

When he reached the outskirts of the village, Januck decided to spend the night on the convent grounds, in a raised granary at the edge of a field. It was a place he and Magda had sometimes played when they were children. But before that he had to find something to eat.

Did he dare sneak into the barn for some milk? He waited. The windows of the main house were dark. Then he flinched and hid himself behind a tree. Several men were coming down the road. The village pub must have just closed.

"We'll show the world. We'll show the world who we are," one of the men blustered.

"Then they'll know," another one said.

"Heil, Hitler," a man at the back slurred.

Januck didn't dare move. He waited until the night was perfectly quiet again, in perfect darkness, then ventured forward.

The barn looked deserted. Maybe the animals had been slaughtered. He opened the door a crack and heard the soft sound of a cow rising to its feet. He was lucky after all, he thought as he looked into the lazy eyes of the bony cow.

The warm milk flowed from the tin ladle into his mouth and he didn't care that some of it spilled down his bushy beard, he was drinking so ravenously. When he'd emptied the ladle he felt sleep begin to spread through his limbs. But first he had to get to the granary.

He climbed up the narrow ladder to the door, where he knew he would have a good view of the convent. He would wait until he saw movement in the yard. Maybe the girls themselves.

Januck wrapped himself in his coat, and before he could even straighten his legs he was fast asleep among the grain.

He spent a few days in this hiding spot and woke with a start one morning at dawn. He could hear someone whispering. It was coming from below him, somewhere in the haystacks.

"I'm going to the front in two weeks," a man's deep voice said.

"Wilfred, I don't want you to leave."

Magda. It sounded like Magda's voice. Januck's brain was alert in an instant, though his body was still numb and stiff, his limbs in knots.

"I promise I'll come back."

"And what about me? I don't want to stay in the convent."

"You can go to the Hitler Youth camp my cousin Ulka runs. Here's the address."

There was a rustle of paper.

"Thank you, darling Wilfred... I will be so happy to get away from..." Magda's voice grew hesitant.

"From what?" the man's voice was low and quiet, like a lurking footstep in the darkness. "Who is it?" Another footstep, closer, slightly louder. "You should tell me everything. You should do your duty for Greater Germany. Do your part, my sweet rosebud."

"There's a girl there. She's a foreigner` and..."

Magda! Be quiet! The command echoed in Januck's head. *Be quiet! Be quiet! Have you gone mad?!*

"And?"

"A Jew. Couldn't you send her away somewhere?"

"Of course."

"Where?"

"There's a clock factory. My Uncle Reinhard is the manager."

"I love you so much, Wilfred."

Januck pressed his hands against his ears, his head rocking from side to side. *No! No!* His head was ringing.

When he lowered his hands, he heard rustling, moaning. He heard her say again and again, "I love you, Wilfred," and Wilfred panting, "My rosebud."

Januck felt disgust flood through him. He pushed his fingers into his ears. If he could, he would have climbed down, but he had to control himself, stay quiet and still, like a coward.

As Januck watched them leaving hand in hand, a chill went through him. He saw the laces of his old hiking shoes, one green, one yellow, swinging along on his sister's feet.

What had happened to Magda?

Januck shut his eyes and clutched his head. He shook himself, as if he were trying to clear his muddy thoughts. They were going to come for Ingria.

Januck climbed down the ladder and took off running. He had to be careful, skirt along the edge of the woods. *Quickly. Quickly.*

He ran down the hill. With each step a stone rolled under his feet. Suddenly he was sliding with a rush down the hillside. He saw sparks, but managed to stay upright. Then he stopped and took a deep breath to calm his pulse. He could see the convent, and in the yard Wilfred. He saw Magda and the nuns and men in uniforms. He saw Ingria get into a jeep. He watched the jeep pull out onto the forest road with Ingria in it, her thin back in a blue blouse between two soldiers as it disappeared around a curve. Januck backed up, deeper the bushes. He couldn't let them see him.

~

The evening darkened and Januck crept through the sheltering trees toward the convent. He stopped, waiting. Listening. Had any soldiers stayed behind to keep guard? The quiet cooing of a lone night bird broke the silence. Januck cupped his hands around his mouth and gave a long, low whistle. It was his and Magda's secret signal to each other when they were children, whenever they were on a hike and one of them disappeared from view. Where are you? the low owl's hoot asked, and the other one would answer with a hoot that said, Here I am. How funny they'd thought it was.

Januck was sure that Magda would recognize the sound. He whistled again. Just a short whistle. A moment later he saw something move on the convent grounds. He was just about to retreat when he heard Magda's answer. The dark-haired girl's silhouette advanced along the cloister wall. Januck stepped out from the trees and watched with tenderness as his sister walked up the slope.

"God Lord, Januck," Magda whispered, staring through the colorless moonlight at her thin, bearded brother.

"I came looking for you and Ingria," Januck whispered.

"It's just me here. Where are Mother and Father?"

"Dead. They're dead, Magda. Everyone's dead. Where's Ingria?"

"I don't know. She ran away."

Januck looked at his sister.

Ran away.

How could she? Anger rose up inside him and blazed like banked embers that could burst into flame at the slightest puff of wind, rage and devour, but in the end leave him wandering, lost in a veil of smoke. *You are a communist, aren't you?* The sudden blow of the interrogator's club, blood shooting from Januck's mouth. He couldn't speak.

"Januck?"

"I saw you with that soldier," Januck said, his voice choked.

"So?"

"Why, Magda?" Januck sighed heavily, as if the grief he felt was more than he could bear.

Magda was quiet, but there was defiance in her eyes. Suddenly, without thinking, Januck said more.

"Be careful you don't create a new life with that beast."

Magda flinched. She stared at him, her eyes dark with fury.

"For God's sake, Magda," Januck said, exhausted. "What's happened to you?"

"Our parents are dead because of you, Januck. You killed them. Because you went over to the side of the communists and the Jews!" The passion in her voice shocked him.

Then they heard footsteps in the cloister yard. Januck ran away and hid in a clump of bushes. He saw Wilfred running up the hill, Magda standing frozen like a statue.

"Who were you talking to? Are you hiding something here?" Wilfred hissed.

"I thought I heard something," Magda said dully.

Wilfred slapped her.

"Who are you meeting behind my back?"

"No one..."

Wilfred grabbed Magda by the sleeve and dragged her back down the hillside.

Januck waited until they had disappeared into the darkness, then he set out again. He had to find someplace else, someplace safe. Magda had chosen her path.

He walked for a while along the road, screened by the underbrush. Then he heard a long, low whistle. Magda. His sister was coming with him! Januck whistled back. But then he heard a car start and drive toward him, the slam of the car door, a dog barking. The tramp of running feet ringing in his ears. Dry branches breaking. Himself, panting. The dog's teeth biting into the skin of his arm. A heavy rock, its weight in his hand striking the dog's snout. Wilfred and his gun. Januck grabbed the gun by its barrel like a ravenous dog grabs a bone. And suddenly, miraculously, the gun was in his hand, pointed at the dog squeaking in pain on the soft ground. And he fired. Out of mercy. He looked at Wilfred for one more moment, at Magda standing behind him.

"Where's Ingria? Where did they take her?" Januck asked.

"Where they take the kikes and your kind," Wilfred answered—and Januck shot him, shot him straight in the place where he knew his heart was. Watched him sag to the ground beside the dog. Everywhere was silence, as if nothing had happened. It was only a moment later, when he heard Magda running away, that he awakened to the sound of the leaves in the trees soughing above him.

The air wrapped around him like a bandage, cooling his burning arm.

~

The next morning the abbess asked Magda to come with her. They descended to the basement. Magda felt a tinge of loathing as she passed the booth were she had performed her penitence, on bread and water.

"This leads to a tunnel," the abbess said, and stooped under a large table that stood against the wall. Magda stared at the thick door.

"The key is in here," the abbess said, removing a stone from the wall. There were also candle stubs and matches there. Magda nodded. "Dear child, if they ever come to get us, run away to the mountains."

She kissed Magda on the forehead.

"I've done something wrong..." Magda began, but couldn't get any more words out.

"No one is pure. We merely strive to be," the abbess said gently.

~

In the morning, Magda awoke to the distant sound of dogs barking. Outside she heard shouts, commands. She dressed for outdoors, silently, tucked the lipstick into her sock and tiptoed down the hallway. She saw the abbess standing with the other nuns in front of a row of Nazis in uniform.

"We don't know anything about a soldier being shot. We are just humble servants of God," the abbess said.

"You are servants of the pope. You take your orders from him, and turn against us!" a young Nazi officer shouted, picked up a gilded, jewel-studded cross from a small table.

"I beg you," the abbess cried, and the cross struck her in the temple.

"Is nothing sacred to you?"

The young man struck her temple again, and she fell to the stone floor.

Magda withdrew around the corner, pulled off her shoes, and crept to the cellar. With some difficulty, she opened the heavy door and locked the latch behind her. The candlelit passageway looked low and narrow. It wound its way upward. After walking for some time, Magda smelled the scent of damp grass and made her way into daylight.

She spent that morning hiding on the hillside, peeping down into the valley, which was bustling with soldiers. Then she saw a truck pull out onto the road, with nuns standing on the truck bed. Their black habits fluttered like mourning flags in the wind.

THE CLOCK FACTORY GIRLS

"Can you imagine them together?" Ingria heard one of the girls behind her ask another as they stood waiting at the door to the factory. She knew the girl was talking about Sybilla and Reinhard. There were giggles, but the line went quiet when Sybilla opened the door.

The work started every day at six. That's when Reinhard appeared in his gray work coat. Ingria didn't think he looked frightening at all. He reminded her of the stooped old watchsmith in Vyborg who never talked much. His underling Sybilla directed their work. She was slightly taller than Reinhard, with a straight back, and her pale eyes always look the same. Her expressionlessness was a torment to Ingria. It was as if Sybilla thought she was a manager at an ordinary workplace, advising each of them in a calm, level voice about how to paint the numbers and the rambling roses onto the clock faces and what kinds of brushes worked best for each phase of the task. The brushes were arranged by number on a rack in front of them. Brush number one was the narrowest. It was used for the dots and the small vines and the veins in the leaves. Sybilla showed them how to hold a brush so that it touched the face of the clock at the correct angle. Then she passed out examples of correctly painted clock dials for them to copy. She said the pattern was based on Swiss clocks. Some of them were console clocks, a style dating back to the mid-1700's, made in the Neuchatel province of Switzerland, Sybilla explained. They painted the clock cases, the numbers, the thorny vines and the little roses. Table clocks and wall clocks. Grandfather clocks taller than they were. Reinhard assembled the clockworks and at night Ingria could still feel the hundreds of clocks ticking, as if she were constantly surrounded by a swarm of grasshoppers. How long would this last? Bozka said they would be there until the war ended.

It would end some day.

Sybilla didn't like Bozka. She was Czech, like Dana. Bozka had broad shoulders and strong calves, like a javelin thrower. She exuded the pungency of the land, the soil. Her slightly sloped eyes looked out defiantly from her broad face and her high cheekbones gave her a daredevil air. Bozka was seventeen. She'd grown up on a large farm and was used to hard work. Subduing the will of the land, altering it so that it yielded its harvest. She was different than the others. She had been taken away in the middle of a day working in the fields, and didn't know why. Her parents had no connection to politics and she wasn't Jewish. Bozka vowed to avenge them. Because she was the strongest of the girls and had large hands, Bozka's job was helping Reinhard carry crates of clocks and wash the paint cups and brushes. The turpentine ate into her skin and gave her blisters. When she asked for hand cream, Sybilla made her scrub the floor of the factory with lye soap and water.

~

When they returned to the outbuilding every evening they fell asleep immediately, and those who were still awake were too numb to care when the padlock on the door clanked, locking them in darkness. They were lost in fear, marked as discards.

"The world has betrayed us. No one is coming," Bozka said one night from the darkness. Dana answered with something in Czech and Katherine asked them to speak German, but Dana said she wanted to at least keep her language. Bozka said that Dana had dreamed of being an artist and Ingria could see how Dana dimmed from the very first weeks, how she watched them all from under her thick eyebrows. Sometimes Bozka would be standing holding the pushbroom and glance nervously at Dana as she sat frozen before a clock face. No one dared show what they were thinking, much less what they were feeling, not with Sybilla's watchful eyes on them. If they did, they would be punished. She had made that clear on the very first morning.

"Everyone betrays someone," Eliza finally said in a thin voice, and that was the last anyone bothered to say about it.

Eliza was a Hungarian Jew. She was fifteen, and she had the dark eyes of the Hungarian steppes, though she was otherwise delicate and pale. Sometimes when she was lost in her own thoughts, she would stare into the distance, and when she did, her eyes were like embers drifting from a camp fire into the night sky, and Ingria would wonder what she was thinking about. Eliza painted as easily as a little finch flies; her hands were slender, her fingers long and thin. Sybilla often stopped and stood behind her to watch her work. Sometimes she gave Eliza lumps of sugar. Eliza would suck on them, her eyes fixed on the clock face in front of her. If Sybilla liked anyone it was her. Eliza was her favorite, a girl who didn't speak and painted rosebuds and vines faster than anyone else.

Ingria wanted to be friends with Katherine from the very first day when she heard at the collection point that Katherine was from Vienna. Katherine was the oldest of the girls; she was already eighteen.

Snuggling up beside Katherine to sleep, Ingria asked her how she had ended up at the clock factory. Katherine whispered that she had been arrested in the middle of the day on her way to a private lesson with a painter. He was a Jew and couldn't get his paintings into the art galleries anymore.

"What about you? How did you end up here?" Katherine asked, her lips close to Ingria's ear.

Ingria shook her head.

"I don't know. Maybe someone found out that my sister was married to someone in the resistance. They were all taken away. My parents, too. Or maybe they knew that I was a foreigner, and that the nuns were hiding me in the convent."

"Any reason will do for them," Katherine whispered. After that they never talked about it again. Months went by before Katherine confided in Ingria. She told her she had been born in London, that she was actually British. The enemy. It was a secret that Ingria couldn't tell anyone.

Maybe it was the way Ingria stared earnestly back at her without any shame, like an artist stares at his model, an appraising, thoughtful look, that finally sealed their friendship.

"What are you thinking about?" Katherine asked her once.

"Your colors," Ingria answered.

"My colors?"

Ingria nodded.

Katherine had long, glowing chestnut hair and calm blue-gray eyes. Nothing seemed to rattle her—not the filthy blankets, though she did give them a long look, or the food they had to eat—burnt potatoes with some sort of sauce, or whatever else they could get. She had the same calm as she stared at the pattern of rose vines and carefully painted them with a thin brush.

They waited for ages in the line to wash up as it inched along, and when Katherine's turn came she would lift the water from the rusted barrel in her cupped hands and rinse her face and neck with such graceful movements that Ingria could only marvel at her calm.

One night Ingria ask Katherine why she didn't cry, why she was never nervous like the other girls. Katherine turned her head and said,

"They wouldn't dare do anything to me. I'm just waiting for my fiancé to settle my case so I can go back to Vienna."

Fiancé?

But Katherine wouldn't tell her anything more about him.

"Not even one thing?" Ingria begged.

And Katherine tilted her head and even her eyes were smiling.

"He's an Englishman." Ingria's eyes asked for more, and Katherine said, "The day we were engaged he read a poem to me. Elizabeth Barrett Browning."

"What kind of poem? "

"Sonnet number 43."

"A sonnet? How does it go?"

"Would you like to learn English?"

Ingria nodded and smiled.

"Listen, Ingria, when I get back to Vienna I'll clear up your case, so you can get out of here."

"And what about the other girls?" Ingria whispered.

"They'll get out, too. This won't last forever. I promise."

And, gazing into Katherine's solemn, blue-gray eyes, Ingria believed her.

~

Once, Katherine said that she had attended boarding school, so she was used to strict discipline. To Ingria, for whom freedom and her wandering mind were one and the same, it was torture to sit under the bright lamps from morning till night painting while outside the colors of the sky we're changing, and her mind longed to be out there. "Where do you think these clocks go?" she whispered once, but Sybilla was walking past behind them, and the girl beside her never raised her eyes from the console clock she was painting. The clocks were unusual because you could hang them on the wall or if you wanted keep them on a table, without any extra support. They had a curved shape that reminded Ingria of a snowman. Katherine told her later that the clocks were given as prizes to Nazis in recognition for their work. How did Katherine always know more than everyone else?

~

When they walked across the yard in the evening dusk Ingria would gaze with dread at the little walled bunker that stood a short distance from the dormitory. The dark smoke from its chimney grew ever thicker every day. When the door of the dormitory had locked behind them, she whispered to Katherine, "What do they burn in there?" Katherine's face quivered, as if in pain. She looked around to make sure no other girls were nearby, then whispered in Ingria's ear, "You saw that the clocks hands are made of gold?" Ingria nodded. "That's where Reinhard melts down the gold."

Ingria didn't understand at the time why that was so secret.

~

The night silence was broken now and then by murmured prayers and snatches of crying from Tekli as she snuggled close to her big sister. Tekli was 12, the youngest, and her sister Iwona was several years older. They were like a large and small version of one another, with their oval faces, thick yellow braids, and big blue eyes. Iwona spoke in a quiet soothing voice to her little sister, words Ingria didn't understand.

There was one evening when they all started singing, every girl in the group. It happened almost by accident. They'd gone to bed after a long day of work and lay quiet, exhausted. Then Tekli started talking. Her small, childlike voice carried from the corner across the room. Ingria didn't understand Polish, so she didn't know what Tekli was chattering about. Iwona seemed to be trying to soothe her. She heard later that Tekli had been talking incoherently. About her mother and father swimming in blood and turning into fishes.

Ingria looked at Katherine. Her eyes were open, too. Then Iwona started to sing a quiet, calming song. Maybe it was a Polish lullaby. When she finished singing, Bozka asked who would sing next. Katherine set up and started humming *The Blue Danube*. Her voice was heavenly—pure and melodious. When she finished, one girl started to clap. And soon others did, too. Ingria could see that Katherine was smiling. Then Eliza stood up and sang a Hungarian folksong. Tekli had stopped jabbering. Someone shouted, "We want Bozka!"

"I don't know how to sing," Bozka said in a low voice, and then, surprisingly, started to whistle. It was a funny little polka, and it made Tekli giggle happily.

"Let's all sing together," Katherine said putting her arm around Ingria.

After that, sometimes on restless nights someone would sing, or they would all sing together. And when they did, Tekli and the other younger girls would fall asleep after the first few bars.

THE MEADOW

With the coming of spring, sunshine blazed on the metal roof of the clock factory and heated the turpentine and paint fumes to a sharp stench that made the girls eyes sting and caused them to cough more than they had before. Tekli passed out first, then Eliza. "Everybody out!" Reinhard shouted. "For half an hour!"

Behind the factory a breathtakingly beautiful sight met them, a meadow full of tall grass and blooming wildflowers, and white mountain peaks visible beyond the forest.

The younger girls picked wildflowers and the older ones wove them into crowns. Bozka twirled around and whistled. Some of the girls ran around the meadow as if in an ecstatic trance. Iwona picked half-green berries and offered them to Tekli, cupped in her paint-stained hand. The color had come back to Tekli's pale skin, and there was a smile on her face.

Ingria sat down beside the little mountain stream that divided the meadow from the woods beyond. The water was cold and clear. It felt good on her aching hands. Katherine came to sit beside her and slid her hand through the sun sparkling water as if she were caressing it. "If there was only this moment, I could forget everything else," Ingria whispered. Katherine looked just like an innocent young woman on a spring day in some old painting. Ingria examined her so carefully that decades later she could still recall that vision of Katherine before her, as if it were that very moment again. The little copper-colored curl of hair wrapped behind her ear, the smooth, pure curve of her brow drawing the soft light to itself, the shining, silken arc of her eyelashes, her narrow wrist glimmering in the water.

Then Katherine tenderly took Ingria's bent, aching fingers in her own, and recited:

How do I love thee? Let me count the ways.
I love thee to the depth and breadth and height
My soul can reach, when feeling out of sight
For the ends of Being and ideal Grace.

Ingria didn't say anything. She didn't want to break the spell, didn't want Katherine's fiancé's words to fly too far away.

~

On another spring day, a little after noon, a rust-spotted car drove up to the factory. It had never come before until after five.

"It's good for the prisoners to get some exercise and fresh air. It has a direct effect on production," Reinhard said to the driver, who looked surprised to see the girls outside moving about. He had brought Reinhard the weekly load of gold. He was a local boy, an idler about 20 years old who had used his family connections to get a job as a courier. His name was Franz. Standing in the factory office, he looked doubtfully at Reinhard and Sybilla, then set a brown canvas bag on the desk. Reinhard picked it up with a broad smile.

"The work is progressing," he said. The bag was heavier than the one the week before, or the week before that. Franz laughed with satisfaction. Sybilla grinned. Then Reinhard opened the bag and shook the gold dental fillings out onto the scale. He wrote down the weight in the designated column in his black notebook and asked Franz for a receipt.

"Till next week," Franz said, returned Reinhard and Sybilla's heil Hitler, and left.

A moment later the car door slammed, its engine started, and the roar of the motor disappeared into the forest. Then Reinhard took out a screwdriver, readjusted the scale to the correct weight, and removed a portion of the gold for himself. He gave one to Sybilla, which she slipped into the pocket of her work jacket.

"For a rainy day if, one ever comes," Reinhard said.

"At some point Franz is going to come and demand

his share," Sybilla said, staring at him with her watery-gray, expressionless eyes.

"He'll get what's coming to him," Reinhard replied.

~

A week later Franz came back, but this time he wasn't alone. The girls in the meadow saw them arrive, five men abreast, crushing the grass under their black boots. Feverish eyes that swept over all of them. The girls froze. The older ones stood with garlands in their hands, the littler ones halted their running. Ingria instinctively pressed herself flat against the bank of the stream and looked out from the tall grass as the men made a run at the girls, like wild things. Flowers flew into the air, the sky bluer than blue bursting as their sharp screams reached up and sliced it open. Ingria waited and waited. It was all going to end, and the men would leave. They would leave. Then she heard a burst of laughter, boots trampling the grass and disappearing behind the factory, the slamming door of the truck, the start of the engine. When she got up, Ingria saw the bigger girls—Katherine among them—lying in the meadow, their paint-spattered work coats around their waists, blood trickling down Katherine's thigh.

Ingria fell to her knees beside her.

"He loves you. Your fiancé," Ingria whispered. "He loves you. He will always love you." but Katherine didn't answer, she just looked up through the clouds.

After that day, Katherine closed up, closed herself

in silence. When they went to bed, Ingria stared at her bent back, the tattered brown blanket pulled around her, sheltering her from the world. Ingria touched her shoulder. Katherine didn't move.

THE RETURN

The men in the black boots stopped visiting when winter came, but once the flowers have risen from the spring soil, they return by the dozen. The older ones wear uniforms, the younger are in civilian clothes. Some of them are mere boys. The oldest man, a balding sergeant, takes the lead. The buttonholes over his bulging gut are strained into wicked grins. His face has a sheen like meat gone bad, his tiny eyes glistening and predatory. Franz follows on his heels, excited, ominously triumphant, glancing at the soldiers on either side of him, some with their jackets already open. The boys from the village are clustered behind them, uncertain, watching the girls stand frozen in place. Bozka has a flower in her hand just picked from the meadow.

The sergeant slaps Franz on the back, looks at the

others and says, "This is what I call a real man!" and casts his tiny eyes on Bozka, who stands stock still holding the flower like a statue in a garden.

The one who grabs Ingria is like any other schoolboy. He's no older than she is, perhaps seventeen. Fair and blue-eyed like the people back home. But this boy is Austrian, and he looks bewildered when he sees that she's afraid. As if he's ashamed, as if he knows that what he's doing is wrong.

He keeps looking around him, his face red. Then the leader of the pack, the pig-eyed sergeant, shouts at him.

"Hans! What are you waiting for? Still too much of a kid, are you?" Ingria hears laughter from someplace behind her.

"Do you need someone to show you how?" the sergeant laughs, and the air trembles with horror. If I don't do it someone else will, Hans thinks frantically. He looks into the girl's eyes, a raging blue storm so dark he can't see the pupils. Neither one of us has any choice, he tells himself, and he says something, it bursts out of him before he has a chance to think. "I'm sorry," muttered into her flaxen hair. Then he shuts his lips, pressing them tight together, and doesn't look at her again. Ingria looks at the birds escaping from the trees and swirling in circles against the sky. Then suddenly she's back and it's quiet. Someone nearby shouts, "Hans," and a weight is lifted off of her. She knows the boy's eyes are trying to reach her, but she looks past him. He looks at the girl whose eyes are bright as an alpine spring on a sunny day, full of beauty, mirrored blue. Even after the war those eyes will follow him, follow him to the end of his days.

Ingria waits. The steps recede. A dragonfly buzzes and stops, as if it's watching her, then disappears in a flash of sunlight on blue and yellow wings. Farther off she hears a muffled bang as the truck door closes, then the engine starting. The sound fades into the forest.

Ingria gets up, not looking around her, walks stiffly to the riverbank and wades to the deepest part of the stream where the water reaches up to her waist, and stands in the icy mountain water until she can't feel anything.

~

The next time the truck comes Hans runs straight to the girl and pushes her down into the wildflowers. And he goes through the motions, pounds against her, rocking back and forth, though she still has her underpants on—and his eyes meet her searching eyes. Because Hans is a captain's son, he can keep her to himself. Every time he's there, he presses a gift into her hand. Chocolate, a piece of cheese, a bag of nuts. Then he's called for deployment. He whispers the news into her ear, sees her eyes fill with terror. "Tomorrow. I leave tomorrow," he whispers into her tangled flaxen hair. It reminds him of a magpie's nest, and somehow it makes her seem even more wounded. Ingria hates the boy, but she needs his protection. Deployment? Maybe the other men of the village will be deployed too. Not just the young ones; all of them. Then she won't—they won't—have anything to fear. This time Hans presses a small package into her hand. "Vitamins," he whispers. He wants to kiss her tender ear lobe, but doesn't dare.

"Thank you," Ingria whispers. She thinks, there's no way he knows that I've been sick. Especially in the mornings. She's pregnant, and is afraid to even think about what's to come. For a moment, she examines the future child's father closely.

"Everyone who's able is going. The village is emptying. I'll help you. I'll think of something." He speaks so quietly that Ingria can just barely hear what he's saying. "What is your name?"

"Amalie Rhein."

"My father is in a high position. I'll help you get out of here."

Ingria believes him. He has an honest face.

"Your eyes are pretty," Hans says clumsily, and thinks, someday I'll come back from the war, and I want to find you.

After Hans left for the front, Ingria believed he must have given some kind of order, because no more outsiders came to the clock factory except for Franz when he came to do business with Reinhard in the office. Although they still glanced fearfully at one another when they went outside on a break, the girls gradually began to believe that the men from the village were finally gone.

~

One hot late-summer day, when Sybilla rings the little bell for break time, Ingria is just finished painting the leaves on a yellow rose vine. She glances at Katherine, who is sitting beside her. There are little beads of sweat on Katherine's pale forehead. Lately the paint fumes make her sick, and her work coat is tight around her middle. Ingria knows what that means, and it seems to her that something bad is brewing in Katherine's mind. Once again, Katherine avoids looking at her.

But then she turns and looks directly into Ingria's eyes. "Do you want to give me a present?" Katherine asks with a feverish look. A present? What does she mean? No one here has anything to give. "Do you?" Katherine asks again, not looking away. Finally Ingria nods. Katherine takes hold of her paint-stained hand and presses it against her mouth. "Give me the gift of a promise. Promise you will never tell anyone anything about me. Or about this." She moves the hand from Ingria's mouth and puts it under her coat, lays it on her mounded belly. "I promise," Ingria says. And Katherine turns and disappears out the door. Ingria wipes her paint-stained hands on her coat and follows the other girls outside.

The heat strikes her face. It spreads over the meadow, quivering, an almost unbearable radiance. Bees frantically circle the bluebells, unable to rest even for a moment; dragonflies whizz back and forth, their wings flashing here and there in the tall grass. Ingria looks behind her. She doesn't see Sybilla anywhere, so she peels away from the group as they scatter across the meadow. Some girls go to the edge of the woods to cool themselves in the shade. Ingria glances at Katherine, but she shakes her head almost imperceptibly. Ingria walks toward the stream. It seems that all the girls want to be alone these days, as if the years have silenced them, taken away their voices. Ingria puts a hand against her swollen belly and lowers herself onto the bank. The stream is sparkling and beautiful with crystal light refracted on its surface, the water clear and cold. It comes straight from the mountains, and feels good on her fingers, which ache more and more every day. Especially her knuckles when she holds tight to the brush. The cold water reduces the swelling.

Ingria lets her hand slide slowly back and forth through the murmuring water, watches the thin trickles of color washing away and vanishing into the water. Then something stops her. Almost like the sound of a car engine. She turns to look but she can't see over the bank to the meadow. She hears voices. Men's voices. Someone laughs. None of the voices sound like Hans.

She presses herself against the sand of the streambank. Lifts her head and sees the men—scruffy men returned from the war. Men who have been to the front, running at the girls like a pack of wolves. They mustn't see me. The thought pounds in Ingria's head, and she presses harder against the ground. "Run into the forest!" It's Bozka's voice. Strong and resonant.

Ingria raises her head warily and peeps between the stems of flowers. Bozka is running toward the forest, her coat flapping behind her, revealing her big belly. Delicate Eliza stares at the running men, her eyes wide, and sprints after Bozka. Katherine's beautiful face is twisted with terror and hate. "Pigs!" she screams, and runs away. Some of the girls freeze, others run. Ingria sees Iwona, holding onto her little sister's hand. Their grasp breaks and Tekli stumbles and falls. Dana's... Suddenly a shot splits the air. Then another. Ingria sees the men stop, stand in the tall grass, aim, fire. She sees Bozka fall. Katherine is shouting, shouting so loud that her voice could reach the village, the back of her work coat colored with blood. Eliza lifts her hands as she runs, as if throwing herself into a stranger's arms as a bullet strikes her narrow back, and she bends and falls across a bush. Bullets come to a stop in tree trunks, between narrow shoulder blades. Ingria presses her head into the sand. Her temple throbs. They mustn't seen me.

Then Reinhard runs outside. His voice echoes beneath the flat blue sky. "Stop!" But the birds fly, and spatter the sky with black.

JANUCK

Januck peered through the fog and could just make out the scattering of farm houses. He had been waiting for hours and nothing had moved, so the sudden shriek startled him. The door of a house flew open and a woman came out screaming in panic.

"Help! Help! Hildegarde is dying!"

From the neighboring house two old women and a youngish one appeared, with sleepy children around their feet, looking on curiously.

"Oh Lord. She's dying. Get help!"

No one moved.

"The doctors are all at the front. You know that," one woman said, picking a little boy up and holding him.

"She's dying!" the woman desperately cried out again.

Januck took a step, then another, and then he was running.

"What's the problem, ma'am? I'm a doctor."

"The baby won't come out," the woman says, her eyes wide with fear. "My daughter. She's dying. And the child, too."

An hour later Hildegarde was lying with the child at her breast, and Januck felt a flicker of happiness.

"How can I repay you?" her mother said.

It took a moment for Januck to muster the courage to look the kindhearted country woman in the eye.

"May I rest here for a few days?" he said.

"Of course. As long as you need to," Hildegarde replied, giving her mother a meaningful look. "Mother, give our guest something to eat"

As Januck was washing up at the well, Hildegarde's mother came and stood beside him.

"We need a doctor around here, if you would like to stay for a while. The slaughterhouse is empty. You could have it all to yourself." Januck nodded and followed her to a building at the edge of the village.

"You can latch the door from the inside," the woman said encouragingly. Januck noticed that the villagers had left a stuffed mattress and a thick blanket for him.

As the days passed, he heard the women whispering, speculating about who he was, and why he was wandering the backwoods. "A deserter. He lost his nerve at the front," he heard one woman whisper, and he didn't say a word. He lanced blisters on the villagers' feet, made sutures from animal gut to stitch up their wounds. Some of them started to call him dumb stick. He was so thin, and never answered.

HANS, 1944

"Someday it will be over," Bozka once said.

Was it over now? The war? The end was coming in any case, closer and closer, day by day. The booming, shaking, sudden flashes that lit up the sky and the whole room. Lit up the faces of the girls and of Sybilla, their expressions frozen.

The nights were the worst. They pressed tightly against one another, listening to each other breathe, to the distant pounding. On one of those nights, from out of the darkness, they heard Tekli singing. She sang in her small, childish voice, the tune that Katherine had once sung to all of them, that they had all sung out together. It's a long way to Tipperary, Tekli sang, just as lustily. Then someone put a hand over her mouth.

~

One day Sybilla ordered them to cover the windows of the factory with blue paper, because of the bombing. It made everything look blue, even their faces. What was going to happen to them? Would a bomb fall on them and wipe them out? Or would someone come—the Americans, the British, the Russians, come to rescue them?

Ingria tried to concentrate on painting the roses, but her hand trembled when the small Blaupunkt radio on Reinhard's desk made its announcements. Reinhard listened, his face tense. That was a good sign, although Ingria could only make out a word here and there through the static: "The battle for Berlin is nearly over... Allies advancing... Russian forces in the east have crossed..."

Ingria saw out of the corner of her eye that a car was pulling up in front of the factory. She cast her eyes downward. Reinhard looked out the window, got up from his chair, and walked outside. Who had he been expecting?

The girls looked at each other nervously

A moment later the front door opened. Something inside Ingria thumped. Rector Bauer. Yes, it really was Rector Bauer. He looked so much older than the last time she had seen him. Five years ago. All the ruddiness was drained out of him; even his dark hair was gray now, and sparse. His sad eyes roamed over the room. Then they stopped at her. Ingria saw his eyes grow wide. What did she look like with her paint-smudged coat, hands dirty, and perhaps her face too, her hair tucked in under its gray rag.

Reinhard stood next to the rector, expressionless.

"Amalie Rhein," Rector Bauer said, "You're being transferred. Orders from the higher-ups."

Ingria felt the other girls watching her. She put down her brush.

"Get up and go with him," Reinhard said drily. As Ingria walked past Reinhard, he put a hand out in front of her. She stopped, and could hardly hear what he whispered to her: "Hans sends his greetings." Then he lowered his arm. When she reached door, Ingria turned and she saw Tekli lift her hand just a little, as if she wanted to touch her. Then the door closed.

A few minutes later she was riding in Bauer's car.

"Didn't your father say that art would save you?" He said, trying to smile.

Ingria had lived for so long in another world that for a moment she didn't understand the question. The time before the war, when she had a father, and a mother, and freedom.

"He said that you should always trust in that. Or did I say that?" Bauer tried to speak in a light tone, to hide his shock; he could see by just looking at her that she had suffered so much.

"My father said art would save me."

"That's right. Now I remember! And I asked you to trust in that. Listen, everything will be alright. You'll see."

Ingria was silent. Where was she being taken?

Bauer peered at her from behind the steering wheel.

"How are you feeling?"

The warmth of that question filled Ingria's eyes with tears, but she had no answer for him.

"You're going to a better place now," Bauer said in a calming voice. "You see, some of the high-ranking officers' wives have a sewing circle or a gossip club or something like that, and they got the idea that the award-winning artist Amalie Rhein should draw their portraits."

Ingria stared out at the headlight beams as they lapped up the dirt road. Hans. Hans had promised to help her. *My father is in a high position.*

"Sometimes in life little miracles happen," Bauer said, and Ingria burst into tears and put her head in her hands. In her mind she saw the baby's little wrinkled fist as it disappeared behind the closing door.

"Ingria, you'll forget your suffering once you see it turned to the good," Bauer said.

They didn't talk after that, just sat silently as the car rolled along a road lined with black spruces.

~

An inn sheltered by snow-covered spruces came into view and Bauer pulled over. He hurried from the car down an icy path to the back door, knocked briskly, and gestured for Ingria to get out of the car and follow.

A large, buxom woman in a house coat appeared in the doorway, quickly looked Ingria over, shook her head, and said the young lady could sleep in the kitchen alcove. Bauer nodded, patted Ingria hurriedly on the shoulder, and whispered, "The war will soon be over," then hastened back to the car, waved, and disappeared into the driver's seat. The next moment his headlights swept over the snowy spruce trees and moved on, leaving darkness behind.

The woman said that her name was Helga Wurst, and that she and her husband owned the inn. She said the officers' wives would be coming soon, perhaps as early as tomorrow, but at the moment the inn was empty except for the two of them because her husband was at the front blasting the Russians, and business was terrible anyway because of the war.

Ingria soon learned that her sleeping place was damp and cold—the inn was short of firewood. And the inn did have other inhabitants, because Ingria started to itch something awful during the night. The next morning Helga Wurst shook her head dolefully, brewed a pungent, smelly tincture, and poured it over Ingria's scalp. She splashed the last part of it into the laundry pot.

While they waited for the ladies to arrive, Helga looked out the window every now and then. Eventually she said that it looked like no models were coming that day, but Ingria might as well use her time to draw Helga. Settling into an armchair in the living room, Helga asked her to include the mountain peaks outside the window in the drawing.

"Now there will be something left of me if we don't make it out alive," she said later as she carried the drawing down to the cellar.

~

Early the next morning, Ingria woke to the sound of shouts outside the house, a car engine, doors slamming. Helga dashed into the kitchen, ransacked the cupboards, and yanked Ingria up from her bed.

Helga scraped some goop from the bottom of a jar with her fingers and smeared it on her face. It smelled like plums.

This should keep their hands off us," she jabbered. "We have to be friendly to them. This is the beginning of the end. They're on the run now. They've come to the mountains looking for someplace to hide." She dabbed a few splotches of jam on her quivering cheeks and neck.

They stood silently side by side and curtsied almost in unison as the men came tromping in. The men looked at them with disgust in their eyes and went into the living room, stamping the snow from their boots. One of them, an officer in a peaked cap, turned back and ordered them into the kitchen. He emptied the canned goods from the cupboards into his knapsack, then closed the kitchen door and locked them in.

From that day into the next there was a steady stream of traffic stopping at the inn. Soldiers arrived in black cars, took wooden boxes out of them and packed them into jeeps that immediately drove away. Ingria and Helga watched it all through a gap in the window curtains. The boxes were probably loot stolen from convents and private Jewish homes—jewelry, gold and silver objects, Helga said, popping a plum into her mouth.

"What they can't drag with them they'll dump in a lake in the Alps," she whispered.

The next day at dawn two men came whooshing into the yard on skis.

"Wilderness guides. They know the mountains better than God himself."

Then the inn doors slammed and the house was suddenly quiet. Men wearing knapsacks appeared in the yard and fastened on their skis, and they all disappeared into the woods, their ski poles slashing little flurries of snow behind them.

"They forgot about us," Helga sighed, as if releasing pent-up pressure. It was only then that Ingria understood the danger.

~

One evening, after they had closed up all the shutters, Helga said, "It's so dark here the devil himself couldn't find us." Night after night they went out in the yard and watched bombs flash over the German side. A few weeks later Helga said it was time for them to hide themselves. Someone would be coming soon.

She pulled back the carpet and lifted a wooden trapdoor.

"This is the root cellar. We'll be safe here if the Russians come first," Helga said.

"Why should we be afraid of them?" Ingria asked.

"The Nazis did terrible things in Russia."

Ingria didn't want to hear what they'd done.

For the next 24 hours they sat, dozed against each other, listened to the shots and explosions, and ate plum preserves until the last jar on the shelf was licked clean.

Then they just waited. They heard thumps and tremors above them.

The floor creaking quietly over their heads.

Ingria felt like she was running out of air, even though there was a draft from a vent near the ceiling. It rained, and a little water dripped from the vent and they took turns pressing their tongues against it to lap up every thin trickle. It was such a meager amount of water that they could hardly gather more than a drop in the bottom of a jar, but Ms. Helga said they should save it for later now that the rain had stopped. She screwed the lid on the jar so it wouldn't evaporate. Ingria wondered how long a person could live without water.

"Hopefully the Americans will find us first," Helga said again, a glimmer of fear in her voice. Then she started to pray in a low murmur, and Ingria pressed closer against her. The thirst made her dream of a sparkling lake with rippling waves like silver silk, and in her sleep she scooped at the soil in the corner and lifted it to her parched mouth. Helga took hold of her wrist and pulled her closer.

When they heard footsteps and squeaking floorboards above them, Helga held her arms so tight that it hurt almost as much as the hunger that chewed at the walls of her stomach. Then someone knocked on the floor with the end of a broomstick or a rifle butt. The person stopped, knocked again right above them, and they waited, watching in terror as the trapdoor was lifted and light streamed in.

IN THE RUINS

"The allies are coming," the group leader Ulka shouted, and ordered them to strike camp. Every box and cabinet had to be emptied before they could leave. Magda had been there ever since the Nazis looted the convent. She didn't know where the nuns had been taken, all she knew was that it had been a long time since anyone had lived an ordinary life, no matter where they were, and she'd had no place to go but the address Wilfred had given her.

Magda held up a swastika flag and looked at Ulka. Secretly, deep down, she hated Ulka. Ulka had betrayed her. They all had betrayed her. Everyone had betrayed her.

"You're just girls who've been here training in various skills, like first aid," Ulka said, and the girls looked at each other.

They carried out everything they could find in the house and piled it in the yard. They took down Hitler's photo and emptied the swastika flags from the cupboards.

"This has never been any kind of group," Ulka stressed. Some of the girls were bewildered and asked where they were supposed to go now, but the leader had no answers for them. "You'll have to take care of yourselves," she said eventually, and shooed them out of the building.

Magda was among the last group of girls to leave. She turned back to look at Ulka, staring at the burning pile. It was all a lie, everything around her.

They walked down the bombed out street, silent, side by side.

When they reached the corner, Magda stopped. "Ulka," she said. It was the first time she had used the leader's Christian name, as if the destruction around them, the heaps of ash, smoldering fires on the sidewalks, chimneys poking out of the ruins had wiped out all formality along with everything else.

"What do you want?" Ulka said, her eyes expressionless.

"Where will I find you?"

Ulka gave her a cold, appraising look, but she wrote her home address and telephone number with a lead pencil in a little black book, tore out the page, and handed it to Magda. Then she walked away, not looking at the smoke and ruin on either side of her,

her back straight, as if she were on her way to the insurance office where she worked before the war.

~

Magda hid out in a demolished house in a suburb of the city. Sometimes the sky flashed but she huddled against a wall like the other homeless did. Among the ragged children was a boy who had escaped from somewhere, but Magda never asked him where. The boy seemed to know everything. He told them about the white buses. The Swedish Red Cross. They had come to take away the Scandinavian prisoners.

They peeked out through the cracks in the walls and watched the long convoy of white vehicles like a parade of ghosts in the dark of morning, headed toward the center of the city. Buses, ambulances, trucks, motorcycles.

Then the convoy suddenly stopped.

German officers surrounded it, SS men and Gestapo. They watched as a field kitchen was set up, and from the buses emerged creatures who just barely resembled people, staggering and stumbling. Their knees were like enormous lumps in their withered legs. The nurses tried their best to keep them standing upright. A draft of wind carried a stench from the doors and windows of the buses to where Magda and the boy were hiding. The German guards walked a distance away and lit cigarettes, watching the scene with sharp eyes.

Magda was baffled by everything she saw. She

whispered almost excitedly, "Do you think more of them will come?"

The boy nodded.

"There are a lot more prisoners. I think the Red Cross is taking them all away. They can't leave the last of the prisoners to die."

The boy was gone from the ruined house the next day, but Magda stayed. She waited for the next convoy, and when it arrived she noticed there were fewer Germans, just a few escort platoons. She worked up her courage and walked to a doctor who was bending over a man lying on the ground.

"Good day," she said with a curtsy. The German soldier guarding the suburb was miraculously indifferent, he just sucked on a cigarette and watched her.

"They killed my parents. Can I come with you and help you?" she asked the kind-looking doctor. "I've had a first aid course." The nurse next to him gave her a sympathetic look.

"What's going on over there?" the German soldier said.

"She's one of us," the brave Swedish doctor replied.

The German shrugged and went back to smoking.

~

In the weeks that followed, Magda fed and gave drink to those too weak to do it for themselves. She bore the stench of vomit and diarrhea. She pushed the cry that rose in her chest down deep, never to be heard. She often slept for just a few restless hours, then started awake. Upon one such awakening she saw an older nurse, Jenny, bent over a man who stared ahead with empty eyes. For a moment Magda thought he was dead, but as she came closer along the narrow aisle she saw that his whole body was covered with boils. Jenny raised her head.

"Can you get me some more cotton balls?"

Magda nodded.

As the two of them dabbed at the man's sores in the silence of the night, he made no complaint, didn't make a single sound. Maybe he was too weak to speak.

"I can stay up and watch him," Magda said once he was cleaned and bandaged.

"Are you sure?"

"Yes," Magda answered. There were dark circles under Jenny's eyes, and she sounded exhausted.

"Come and fetch me if you need help."

When Jenny had left, Magda looked over the patients. They all seemed to be asleep.

The steady hum of the bus made her eyelids heavy, but she forced herself to keep them open, staring out the window at the trees and bushes flitting past, the random twinkling lights. To stay awake she pinched herself now and then on the arm so hard that it hurt and left a red mark.

Suddenly a British plane dove out of the sky, and disappeared just as quickly behind the clouds. Magda stared into the black sky.

Then she felt her head nodding. Had she fallen

asleep? She looked around. Perhaps for just a minute or two. She looked at the patients' faces.

She noticed a young man bathed in sweat whose lips were moving. His chest was covered in a broad white bandage.

Magda got up and went over to him, wiped the sweat from his brow with a damp rag.

He opened his eyes and said something in Swedish.

"What's the matter?" Magda whispered.

"I want to leave," the man said, in German now. "I want to leave Austria. I have to hurry."

There was pain in his eyes. Insistence.

"We're on our way. We're leaving."

"Agnes is waiting for me," the man said, and closed his eyes. Magda saw then that his bandage had turned red with blood. She looked around frantically and sputtered, "Soon. You'll be home soon. Agnes…"

Then she saw his gaze freeze as life left him.

III

OTHER PORTRAITS

Ingria sat with her sketchpad. An American sergeant sat opposite. He asked her in a friendly voice if there was anything she needed. Ingria shook her head. "I have it all in my memory, thank you," she said.

And she drew. She drew all of them: Reinhard, Franz, Sybilla, the village men, everyone who came there. Except Hans. She tried, but her hand wouldn't obey her. It kept stopping, every time.

What happened there? they asked her, but she just stared with wide eyes at them. She had no answers. She drew a forest full of girls, their backs to the viewer. When they asked her about the drawing, she mumbled, "Forest maidens."

"What happened at the clock factory?" they asked again, in a quieter, slightly more demanding tone.

"We painted clocks," she said finally, because

the questioner was now Alice, a friendly, gentle-eyed American.

Alice looked for a long time at the drawing. She had the patience to wait for Ingria's answer, and Ingria told her more, opening the door just a little, giving her a look inside, a little more each time, and a little more, until everything was written down in the report. But Katherine was still behind the door, hidden. Shhh, Katherine whispered. Ingria wanted to tell them about the day the birds flew, spattering the sky with black, but the maidens disappeared into the forest and refused to turn around.

Ingria turned and walked to the office door, with Alice's thoughtful gaze on her back. She needed time, Alice thought, but out loud she said that Ingria was welcome to come and see her whenever she liked. Ingria turned and nodded, then walked out of the room into the polished hallway, where the young sergeant looked up from his desk with raised eyebrows, questioning. But Ingria didn't care about the answers, and kept walking, out through the high doorway into the hard, white light of day. *The baby's fist disappearing behind the door.* Ingria hurried her steps

~

She was accumulating quite a stack of portraits. She drew all the men in the jeep, the men who came to the convent. She drew Sister Elke and the abbess, the blind singer, the men and women at the meeting place, the men who took them to the clock factory and the ones who set out from the inn into the mountains… Her hands were covered in chalk pastel dust. The joints of her fingers ached. The doctor who examined her said that her body had begun to consume the calcium in her bones to survive. The American sergeant brought her a big glass of warm milk without being asked. She drank it greedily. From time to time the sergeant asked her if she needed anything. She shook her head and he brought her another glass of milk. She couldn't keep anything else down yet.

For years she had never seen herself in a mirror, not until the Americans came to the inn and opened the trap door. She knew she was thin, but when she looked in the big mirror in the dark hallway that day, what she saw took some getting used to. Her hair hung in thin, drab tufts on either side of her face, like remnants of tattered lace. There were itchy bald patches on her head, until they gave her a medicated rinse to kill the lice. Her collarbones stood out like the polled horns of a scrawny cow.

Her ribs were so clear you could count them.

~

The sergeant who brought the milk was named Benjamin. Ingria thought the name sounded like a soft feather pillow that she longed to lay her head on. She sat down again on the folding metal chair and opened her sketchpad. She didn't notice Benjamin watching her from behind his pile of papers. His lips curled in a smile, but it was a kind smile, as if there was something funny about Ingria's compulsion to draw, her hands trembling with each fevered stroke of the chalk.

Benjamin had never watched someone draw up close, had never met a single artist. He felt shy, and kept going into the back room to warm her some milk on the spirit stove. He was glad when the peculiar girl started to show signs of gaining weight. One day he came to find Ingria's chair empty and was filled with uneasiness. Several hours later Alice's office door opened and Benjamin looked up and said hello, but Ingria walked right past him with Alice beside her, head hanging. They disappeared out the front door. Benjamin didn't go to lunch. He waited. Alice came back alone and closed herself up in her office.

Ingria had learned from Alice that her family was dead, that she no longer had a home in Vyborg, because the city belonged to the Soviet Union now. She was gone for two weeks. Benjamin lifted his head every time the door opened, but didn't see Ingria. Then she came back, sat down on the folding chair, and started to draw.

He saw her sister, her mother, her father. "We came to Austria together," Ingria said, and gave the drawings to the archive. Maybe someone would be able to tell them something about what had happened to them. Then she drew Januck, Magda, and Mr. and Mrs. Waldermann. She remembered the square man at the cemetery, Januck's friend. The man at Heldenplatz with the icy stare. Maybe someone will know something, Ingria said, and handed Benjamin another bundle of pictures.

The people in the pictures look healthy and

prosperous, and Benjamin couldn't bring himself to say that no one would likely have seen them like that. The first photos from the war had been developed—the liberated prisoners in striped uniforms, emaciated, their hair and teeth gone, the piles of bodies.

As Benjamin leafed through the drawings, he thought about what Ingria's drawings told him of the Waldermann's home, where these innocent people in their lovely clothes ate pancakes and talked and laughed and listened to Chopin played on the piano by a young man in love, to cheer up his mother-in-law.

How was all that destruction possible?

~

Alice turned off the bright overhead light and adjusted the blinds. She was waiting for Ingria, the labor camp survivor. The girl artist who couldn't talk about what had happened to her. Or what had happened at the clock factory. A quiet knock at the door. When Alice opened it, Ingria looked past her, as if searching for something, but Alice knew that it came from fear, that she wanted to be sure it was safe to come in.

"Please sit down," Alice said quietly, pointing to two chairs that stood side by side against the wall. In front of the chairs was a table with a stack of paper and a box of chalk pastels. Ingria seemed to consider for a moment which chair to sit in, then chose the one nearest the door.

"Would you like to tell me about the other girls at the clock factory?" Alice asked. She waited calmly for an answer, sitting in a worn old leather chair. The sunshine filtering through the blinds created a friendly half light around them, and Alice hoped it would make Ingria forget that they were sitting in a low office with whitewashed concrete walls. Ingria sat stiffly on the edge of her chair. The ticking of the clock on the wall filled the silence. Alice rose, took the clock down from the wall and put it in her desk drawer. Ingria's tight shoulders lowered. Alice put her hands calmly in her lap and waited.

"You don't have to talk about it if you don't want to," she said finally.

They sat for a moment, and Alice asked, "Would you like to draw something?"

Ingria nodded, hesitated a moment, chose a pink pastel, and sat looking at the blank paper.

RECTOR BAUER

Rector Bauer sat in the large leather armchair. He
hadn't been in his old office in years. From where
he sat he could see the park, though the window was
covered in gray dust. He couldn't distinguish the statue
of Schiller or the green of the trees. Everything was
the same gray uncertainty.

He felt sadness, with no precise object for the
sorrow. Perhaps his melancholy was due to the lost
beauty, to the fact that everything that had once made
him happy was gone.

His thoughts wandered to the vanished works
of art that a group of American soldiers had been
sent to search for. They had already found some of
them. Others were still missing, and some would
never be found because the Nazis had burned them
as degenerate art.

Bauer lit a cigar. He'd found it in the desk drawer. He didn't know who left it there, and didn't care. Nor who had left the remains of a bottle of cognac he'd found in the file cabinet. He just poured himself a substantial shot in a glass he'd found.

He breathed in the stinging cigar smoke. Life in these times seemed like some sort of half truth. What all was still before them, he didn't dare even think about. Then he heard footsteps echoing down the corridor and climbing the broad stone steps. Coming closer.

He heard a knock. The smell of the cigar must have made its way into the corridor.

"Come in," he said, not knowing who could have wandered into this bombed, dust-filled place.

"Ruth!" Bauer shouted when he saw his old secretary. He was so happy that he ran to the door where she stood, thin and tall. He shook Ruth's hand, and her bony face receded into a smile, revealing the years lost somewhere. Bauer laid his hand on her shoulder.

"What a pleasure to see you, sir" Ruth said, wiping the corner of her eye and begging his pardon for her show of emotion.

They looked at each other for a moment, like two people who had miraculously survived a war and couldn't fathom why fortune had favored them.

"Cognac. I found some cognac. Quality stuff," Bauer said, feeling the happiness that he had a moment earlier thought lost. He fetched another glass and poured some for Ruth. He averted his gaze from her arm, the tattooed number there.

"To life," Ruth said, and lifted the glass to her lips.

"To life," said Bauer, emptying his glass.

"There's a lot to do here." Ruth set her drink down and looked around.

INGRIA AND BENJAMIN

One day Ingria shoved her sketchpad into her canvas bag, wiped the chalk dust from her fingers, and told Benjamin that she had drawn everything. Working up his courage, Benjamin asked her to go for a walk with him. He saw a little smile on her face, in her eyes. "I'll pick you up after work," he said.

They walked along the Danube River, not very quickly, because Ingria was easily winded, and her joints and muscles ached.

"Shall we sit down on a bench?" Benjamin asked. Her striking blue eyes turned to him, and he was overcome with the feeling that he would do anything to make her happy.

Benjamin was 23 years old; he had never planned his life out very far. Both his parents were teachers, and rather old. They weren't his biological parents. He had been adopted from Canada. That was all he knew about his origins. He didn't really know what else to say to Ingria, and didn't dare ask her about her experiences. He just took her hand, gently caressed it, and wondered whether she would want to come with him to Pennsylvania. To marry him.

Marry.

The thought of it nearly made him stop his caresses. He was almost certain to get his old job back at the surveyor's office. And they could move into a place downtown until he had enough money for a little house in the suburbs. For a moment he could see Ingria there, sitting in the yard behind the little wooden house with her sketchpad in her hand, stroking the dreamy-eyed cat sitting beside her.

"Do you like cats?" Benjamin asked, slightly embarrassed by the dreamy hint of the fantasy in his voice.

Ingria smiled and nodded. "Why do you ask?"

"No reason. I like cats, too. And gardens."

"There is something soothing about them."

Benjamin nodded.

"Shall we go back?" Ingria asked. The wind blew little wakes that moved across the surface of the river.

Benjamin rubbed her arms to warm them, and they stood up.

The wind was stronger now, fluttering Ingria's thin skirt.

FROM STOCKHOLM
TO VIENNA

L ooking out the window of the train from Sweden to Austria, Magda saw cities bombed to rubble, villages destroyed, bodies floating in the lakes.

"There are so many of them, the victims of the bombings," she said in a low voice to the woman across from her, who was also staring out at the lake. The woman lowered her eyes. Magda felt she had said something inappropriate, but then the woman replied, with a slight break in her voice, "Those are men and women who committed suicide."

Magda gave her a questioning look.

"They woke up to the Nazis' great betrayal... Or perhaps they could no longer live with themselves," the woman said.

The train veered closer to the lake. Magda saw

among the bodies that had drifted ashore children tied together, old enough to swim. She turned away.

After that they didn't speak. They had no words to say. They listened to the rumble of the train.

~

In the afternoon Magda arrived at the village where Wilfred's uncle Reinhard had his clock factory. She was looking for Ingria, and she knew that after this trip was finished she would never again return to Austria.

At first the villagers told her there was no clock factory. But she persevered with her questions, because she didn't believe that Wilfred had lied to her. *That's where they're taking them. To paint clock faces.*

She offered a stooped old man a bundle of money for answers. He looked at her with small cold eyes, spit and said that snoops like her shouldn't come poking around. Then he hobbled away.

The whole village seemed to be keeping quiet about it.

At the corner store, some children stared at her, curious.

"Do you know who is the oldest person in this village?" Magda asked a little girl, smiling and holding out a piece of Swedish chocolate she had brought with her from Stockholm. The girl looked at the foil wrapped candy for a long time, then finally pointed to a small cottage at the edge of the field.

"The witch," she said, taking the piece of chocolate. "She lives in the blood house." Then the little girl ran away

Magda set off along the path between field and forest.

There was no one in the yard. The wire fence around the abandoned chicken coop had a man-sized hole in it.

Magda knocked at the cottage door.

After a moment she heard the floorboards creak, and the door opened. A little old woman stood there. Her skin was flaking, her gray hair had an oily sheen, and her bare scalp was covered with seeping boils. There was dried food down the front of her tattered blouse.

"What do you want?", the woman said, leaning on her cane.

"I want to talk about the clock factory."

"Do you have any cigarettes? American?"

This too was among Magda's provisions. She knew that they could be used as currency when crossing borders.

She took a pack of Camels out of her purse.

The woman turned and Magda followed her inside. Fetid air struck her in the face. She looked around. A large pot covered with soot stood on the woodstove. Dirty rags were strewn across the floor. Magda remained standing. The old woman sat down at a large, high wooden table. There was something ghastly about the place. The woman lit a cigarette. She sucked the smoke in greedily and look at Magda.

"They all took off, and burned the factory down when they went. That's why it's not there anymore. It was over at the end of Meadow Road."

"Where did the girls end up?"

"The clock factory girls..." the old woman said slowly. "That's what the men called them. They liked visiting there."

Liked visiting there. Magda felt a wave of nausea.

"What happened to the girls?"

"Worse things to some, better things to others," the woman said. "But I wasn't to blame. They were just so weak, on those rations. Reinhard decided who could give birth and who couldn't. Some of them needed to be aborted. They weren't going to make it to term. Especially the youngest girls. I was just doing my job."

"The girls had children?" The thought was so devastating that the shock showed on Magda's face.

The old woman cackled with a toothless grin. Magda stared at her in horror. When her laughter had ebbed she peered at Magda with crafty little eyes.

"What do you expect, with the men coming to visit? They sent the babies to the inspection station. The best ones were sent to nice homes, with high-ranking officers. But only if they were blond, blue-eyed, and healthy. The Lebensborn, that's what they called it... Who are you looking for?"

"Ingria Silo's child."

The old woman gave a guffaw.

"Those prisoners didn't have any names."

"She had blonde hair, almost white, and her eyes were very dark blue."

"They had one like that," the old woman said, puffing smoke into the air. She gazed off into the distance. "And that girl did have a baby. I remember it."

"She did?" Magda said tensely, but softly, not wanting to disturb the old woman's memories.

"That girl fought so hard it took two men to hold her down. She wrapped her arms around her belly, as if she could keep the baby inside. Screamed and shouted, but nobody could understand what she was saying. She spoke some strange language... Finnish, I think somebody said."

"What happened to her?"

"What happens to everybody in a war? People die," the old woman said, more perky now. She stubbed out her cigarette on a dirty plate. "Nobody got out of that clock factory alive when the war ended."

"What about the baby?"

"Got another pack?"

Magda took out another pack and handed it to her.

"The truck driver knows. You should ask him."

"Who is he?"

"He might be dead. The dead don't talk," the old woman laughed, rocking herself. Magda took hold of her hand. "His name. I want to know his name," she said, squeezing the woman's wrist, hard.

"Dieter Hause. He went to Vienna."

Magda let go. The old woman spit on the floor and stared dully at her, and Magda walked out of the house.

She still had a few hours before the train left, so she turned her steps to where the factory once stood.

When she reached the end of Meadow Road she stopped and looked around. Among the overgrown grass there were concrete foundations. She sat down on one. Some distance away, at the edge of the forest, flowed a mountain stream. The meadow was filled with flowers.

Magda listened to the silence, the hum of a bee, the sudden call of a bird in the woods, deep in thought. She bent to run her fingers through the grass.

Something shiny flashed among the stems. Perhaps a hiker had lost a button. She pushed the grass aside and picked up a small lump of gold—a dental filling. Magda turned her head away. A wave of sickness rose from the pit of her stomach and overflowed onto the ground.

~

Dieter Hause heard the doorbell ring. Was it another official with endless questions he didn't know how to answer? Finally Dieter went and asked through the door, "Who's there?"

A woman gave her name. Said she had come on a personal matter.

He opened the door just to get a look at her. Magda asked if she could come in.

He let her pass and waved her into his humble room. She said she would only stay a moment.

He had a guess who she might be. She was dressed in a smart jacket and a cocked, brimmed hat. He took note of her silk stockings and elegant strapped shoes. The woman pulled the thin gloves from her hands and laid them on the table.

"I'm looking for a particular child," Magda said, and noticed the young man flinch. "It's not my child, and I don't mean to cause anyone any trouble. I just want to know where the child is."

Magda opened her purse. She took out a pack of Lucky Strikes, took out a cigarette, and offered one to Dieter. He gave her a light from a brass zippo that smelled of gasoline.

"There were a lot of them," Dieter said in a weary voice, blowing out smoke.

"This was a Finnish girl's child," Magda said.

Dieter remembered the baby. A chubby, healthy one. The quack who delivered it thought it was a miracle, considering what the mother had been fed at the clock factory.

"I was ordered to take the child directly to a Mr. and Mrs. Hartz. Apparently they had been waiting for a child for a long time. Usually they take the baby to be weighed and measured first."

"Do you remember where they lived?"

"On Strassergasse. In a white, villa sort of house. The woman's first name was Yvonne."

"Do you remember anything about the workers at the clock factory? What happened to them?"

Dieter looked at her for a long time. He didn't want to get mixed up in anything, and kept his mouth shut. There were a lot of rumors at the time, rumors that the factory had been blown up, and the workers killed.

"I'm just a driver," he answered, as he had many times before.

The young man's face was closed. Magda got up and thanked him, left the pack of Lucky Strikes on the table, and walked out.

~

When she came to the white house, Magda slowed her steps. This was the second day she'd walked past, walked around the block where Mr. and Mrs. Hartz lived with their little daughter. The house looked clean and quiet. Spotless, as if every bit of dust and dirt had been washed and scrubbed away. The lawn was cut low and even. It was a little world surrounded by a white stucco fence.

When she had walked around the block three times, she saw Yvonne Hartz come out of the house carrying a little blond girl with a bow in her hair. The little girl had a block in her hand, which she threw in the grass. The woman called her Grete. As Magda passed the gate she saw the woman smiling, the little girl running toward her with the block in her hand again. "Mutti! Mutti!" the girl shouted. The woman smiled a broad smile of pure happiness, pure joy. Then Mrs. Hartz looked up and noticed the strange woman standing on the other side of the fence staring at her and at her child, and Magda hurried away.

THE GIFT

Ingria walked along the windy banks of the Danube, a book pressed against her chest. A few weeks ago Benjamin asked if there was anything she might like to have. Silk stockings? Chocolate? Ingria said, A book.

Whenever anything surprised Benjamin, he lowered his head until his chin touched his chest and his sparkling eyes bulged just a little in astonishment.

"Yes, a book. *Sonnets from Portuguese*," Ingria said. She didn't think such a book could even be found, but a few weeks later he'd handed her a thin volume wrapped in paper.

And now she held the book tight against her side, sat down on the bench, and brushed her windblown hair from her face.

She opened to the first page. She read until the

light began to fade, the day darkening to evening. She reached sonnet 43 and read it to the end:

I love thee with the breath,
Smiles, tears, of all my life! —and, if God choose,
I shall but love thee better after death.

Ingria closed the book. She shivered. The wind puffed up her skirt. The lead-gray water of the river made restless movements, as if it wanted to escape somewhere and couldn't find anywhere to go. Ingria listened as it splashed loudly against the shore.

Katherine who? The woman at the office had asked her in a tense voice.

I don't know her last name. She had a fiancé. An Englishman.

The woman closed up the record book and looked sharply at her over her spectacles.

Next! she called, her voice falling cold onto the counter.

~

One evening Benjamin came to her door. This time he had a package wrapped in brown paper. His face was happy and excited.

"Come in," Ingria said, and walked with him into the dim room. He had brought chocolate the last time. Ingria was visibly returning to good health, though she was still pale. And sometimes in her own world. But that didn't bother Benjamin. He was an easy-going young man with a healthy color in his face, and happy, friendly eyes. He felt an eager anticipation every time they met. Their meetings were like buoy markers in the open sea of this strange city. He sometimes wondered what Ingria did all those hours when they weren't together. He knew that he was the only guest who visited her in her corner room at the boarding house. The last time he had visited he noticed a new drawing hanging on the wall. It was a portrait of a young woman with long auburn hair and calm blue-gray eyes. The woman was crouched down with one hand in a flowing stream. He decided not to ask who she was. He had learned not to ask prying questions, because Ingria might unexpectedly withdraw into her shell.

"I brought you something," Benjamin said excitedly, and handed her the package.

Ingria smiled shyly and thanked him.

She sat down calmly in a chair and began to open the brown paper with her slender fingers. Benjamin knew that she had arthritis in her middle finger and that was why it was crooked. It took her a moment to get the knot untied. When the fluffy, pale-colored overcoat was revealed Ingria looked surprised and Benjamin, unable to wait any longer, got up and helped her put it on.

"You are the most beautiful thing I know," he said.

He suggested they go for a walk. Outside on the sidewalk, he wrapped an arm around Ingria's shoulders and said, "They're sending me home in three weeks. They're shipping us to New York, and I'll go from there to Pennsylvania."

Ingria listened to the sound of their footsteps.

"Would you like to come with me?" Benjamin asked.

THE CARE CENTER

After the war ended, Januck tried to get used to his new life at the psychiatric hospital. The name of the place, the War Casualty Care Center, made his skin crawl. He was still a doctor after all, and he had all his limbs and wits about him. His spirit was what was broken, he understood that. So he took his psych medication and sank into mental numbness, where he was not haunted by the ghost of Margit, or anyone else.

In the dining hall, the same glum glee club always sat at the same long wooden tables. The German physics professor Maximilian sat on his right, and across from them sat the Austrian theologian, who Maximilian called Hinge, because of his creaky voice, and next to Hinge sat the Biologist.

Januck didn't yet know Maximilian's story, but he suspected it was the same as everyone else's, all his close relatives dead, and not from natural causes.

They ate in silence.

"Don't you like carrots?" Januck asked Maximilian. He had noticed that Maximillian often left them uneaten.

"Hitler was a vegetarian," Maximilian said, pushing the stewed carrots to the side of his plate.

"They used to bring in tasters, including a 14-year-old girl, a relative of mine, to make sure his food wasn't poisoned."

Januck didn't ask what happened to the girl. He chewed up a piece of stewed cabbage, felt it's soggy mass against his palate, the thick veins of the leaf, and swallowed with some difficulty.

Maximilian told him more about the girl later. They were sitting in the reading room of the care center, an autumn storm outside. There was a rather wide selection of donated books in the reading room, mostly old textbooks, works of philosophy and poetry, but also novels. There were also major domestic and international newspapers and a few magazines, paid for with a portion of the War Victims Rehabilitation Society funds. Patients should have information about what was happening in the world, it had been decided after some discussion, though it was agreed that war photos could cause nightmares, so the most explicit ones we're clipped out before the publications were put in the reading room.

Januck could always find something to read there. Having nothing better to do, Maximilian amused himself by going through the physics textbooks, which were to him as crosswords are to other people, though he rarely needed a pen, preferring to work the answers out in his head. The books made available to them were harmless ones.

They sat next to each other at the long wooden table, the wind now and then tossing handfuls of rain against the window. Januck was reading a book called *The Haunted Heroes of Eugene O'Neill*, Maximilian a book on quantum theory. How this book on O'Neill's plays had ended up out here in the woods Januck didn't know, but books sometimes have unexpected trajectories. Maybe some American soldier who was a drama enthusiast had left it there. In any case, he had a moment earlier run his finger along the spines of the books on the shelf and stopped at this one, because it piqued his curiosity. Though he knew nothing of O'Neill's plays, he had immediately recognized the name and knew that he was a great American playwright whose works were performed in Europe as well. The flyleaf was inscribed:

Men still need their swords
To slash at ghosts in the
Dark. Men, those haunted heroes!

Lazarus Laughed, Act Three Scene One

He took the book and sat down to read it. He had only read a few pages when Maximilian suddenly said, "They killed them all. All the girls who were tasters, except one, who escaped when the red army arrived.

She wasn't my relative."

One day here was much the same as another, measured out in the same morning porridge, the same lunch and dinner. Some things did change, but in the outside world. The men here had fought their own war.

~

The Biologist was surveying the birds, writing down the country, region and time where each bird was banded with a stub of pencil in a little notebook. Januck sat on a long bench next to the building, watching him. The Biologist was holding a bird in his hand with a sure grasp, talking to it.

"I'm just about to let you go free. Don't worry," he said, and lifted his head, which was swathed in a thick fur cap.

"This *Erithacus rubecula* was banded in Tammisaari, Finland." Januck's face revealed nothing. He got up and went inside and the Biologist continued busying himself with the birds. Januck went to his room and closed himself up within its walls. He spent some time with memories of Margit and came out only when the pretty nurse Fleimar came to coax him.

"It's a beautiful winter day," she said from the other side of the door.

On that beautiful, icy, crystalline day Januck, Maximilian, and Hinge kept company with the Biologist, whose cheeks were nipped by the cold. They sat side by side on the long bench in winter hats and thick winter coats. Before them lay a landscape that each of them knew by heart: the rowan trees and poplars, the larches farther off, and beyond them the spruce. There was no world beyond that, not like there was for other people.

"*Erithacus rubecula*," the Biologist whispered. They watched the red-breasted robin hopping along a frosty branch. Now and then the bird turned its head and looked at them, as if it were performing for an important audience, flicking its tail flirtatiously and winging from branch to branch.

Maximilian liked to talk about Freud and Einstein's correspondence. "The book"—by which he meant *Warum Krieg?*, or *Why War?* —"was written and published before the second world war. In 1932, in fact."

"There have always been wars. It is human nature to want to fight. No one can eradicate it," Hinge said, beating his hands together to warm them.

"Our arms should be weapons of the spirit, not shrapnel and tanks," Maximilian quoted, his voice majestic now. After that they were quiet, each in his own thoughts.

Suddenly the Biologist took something out of his pocket and tossed it—a piece of ginger bread he had stolen from the coffee cart.

The *Erithacus rubecula* flew toward them, looked at the Biologist, who sat smiling with his nearly toothless mouth, and snapped up the gift.

"I'll catch him next time," the Biologist said.

Maximilian, whose nose was red with cold, turned and looked at him.

"What for?"

"I want to find out where it was banded."

~

The next day, Januck watched the Biologist out of the corner of his eye and saw him staking out the coffee cart, waiting for the moment when Fleimar had her back turned. Then his hand shot out, quick as a housefly, and a gingersnap disappeared into his pocket.

"This particular gingerbread has ground peanuts in it. *Erithacus rubecula* is especially fond of them. Would you like to come with me?"

So Januck and the Biologist sat outside in the darkening evening in their thick, gray wool ulsters and matching caps with brims and earflaps, bought by Head Nurse Knauss from a mail order catalog.

Sitting on the bench, they heard a tick tick tick coming from beyond the trees. The Biologist screwed up his mouth, which he had a habit of doing when he was particularly pleased about something.

'It's coming," he said, and nodded in such a way that the brim of his hat formed a sharp curve like the broad beak of a bird, and a little cloud of steam puffed out of his mouth. They sat silent and listened to the faint, beautiful sound. Tick tick tick.

The robin flew and landed at the Biologist's feet and he held out a hand filled with crushed gingerbread. Januck waited as if he were watching an exciting play. Suddenly the *erithacus rubecula* hopped onto the palm of the Biologist's hand and, glancing now and again at the man who held it, pecked at the bits of gingerbread.

ULKA

Magda let the telephone at the other end of the line ring seven times, the eight.

It was a two-story house, and the phone was downstairs.

"Hello?" Ulka answered, a bit breathlessly. In the background, in a dark corner of Ulka's living room, her father, a former SS officer who had lost his hearing in an explosion during the war, dozed in his armchair. He opened his eyes and quickly closed them again.

"This is Magda."

Ulka wasted no time. "I destroyed as many papers as I could when I left the camp. I don't know if your information was among them. But no one has come asking about us. Not yet," Ulka said. She sounded nervous.

"What about the photograph?"

"I did get a photograph of her," Ulka said. She didn't like long telephone conversations about the past and didn't want to attract attention to herself, but Magda had sent her enough money that she had agreed to go and photograph the little girl, Grete. She didn't know who the girl was, but she had learned to keep her mouth shut about everything.

"It will take a few days to develop the picture, because I can't go running around the city when my father needs constant care," she said. There was restrained anger in her voice, even bitterness.

Before Ulka went back to her chores, Magda asked her something she had wanted to know for a long time:

"Did you ever find out what happened to the girls at the clock factory?"

"Reinhard destroyed all the lists of names. They're simply gone."

Gone.

"Why?"

"Do you even need to ask?"

Magda made no reply.

"Hello?"

"I'm going to be moving away from Stockholm."

Ulka promised to send the photograph as soon as she got Magda's new address. Then the line went dead.

Magda picked up her small suitcase and joined the throng of people making their way towards the ship. Among the crowd were people she recognized, freed prisoners she had seen on the white busses. They didn't want to stay in Sweden, didn't want to go back to Austria or to Germany. They wanted to leave their sorrows behind. There were others, too, hopeful people departing for a new continent, waving happily to their families from the deck. No one had come to see Magda off. She walked up the gangplank with her back straight, the past behind her.

> *What do they talk about at home?*
> *Where does your brother go? Who does he meet?*
> *He goes to Café Hawelka to meet his friends.*
> *And to Grinzingen cemetery.*
> *What do the adults at home talk about?*
> *About Hitler. They don't like him.*

When she found her cabin, Magda left her luggage there and went out onto the deck for some fresh air. She leaned against the railing and looked at the harbor. The ship floated away from the land as if from a giant's kick and the shore receded farther and farther until the well-wishers with their waving hands looked like tiny, colorful dots. Magda shivered in her thin jacket. She turned and went back inside.

SIMON

"Coffee?" Nurse Fleimar said, picking up a mug from the coffee cart.

Januck nodded and smiled. With his coffee he got a few gingersnaps on a paper plate. They had stopped using real China when a survivor of Auschwitz had ended his days with a broken plate.

"Two sugars, isn't it?" Fleimar said, her large, smiling doe eyes shining.

Januck nodded several times and looked around at the men sipping their coffee. Wounded souls, every one of them. Should they be happy to just be alive? So many others died.

Januck looked at his brother survivors: the Biologist, who in his terrors had lost his name and dedicated all of his energy to his friends, the birds. Maximilian, wasting his genius looking at dated textbooks out here in the woods. Hinge, mumbling Bible verses to himself. What good did it all do anyone?

"Why are you staring at me?" the Biologist asked. Januck awakened from his thoughts.

"I hope we're remembered one day," he said.

"We've already been forgotten," Maximilian shouted.

When coffee time was over, Januck went to talk to Fleimar. He asked for permission to go to Vienna.

She gave him a probing look.

"Where in Vienna do you plan to go?" she asked.

"I want to go visit a friend of mine."

No one had come to visit Januck, and Fleimar raised an eyebrow, meaning she would like to know more.

"His name is Simon. Simon Wiesenthal. We were both at Mauthausen concentration camp at the same time. He's often mentioned in the newspapers," Januck added vaguely, his gaze wandering.

Fleimar had also read the newspapers, and she knew that Wiesenthal was collecting information about Nazi crimes for the trials at Nuremberg.

"I'll ask the head nurse," she said. "Wait a moment please." And she disappeared down the corridor.

She was gone a long time, and Januck was sure she was discussing the matter with the psychiatrist.

While he waited he watched a patient chattering to himself and swinging his fists at some invisible enemy as he padded down the hallway. Some of these men would never survive outside the care center's walls. Fleimar returned.

"Yes, we can arrange it, but you have to be back before evening coffee."

~

Januck had a novel feeling of freedom riding the bus to Vienna. He saw familiar buildings outside the window—government offices, church steeples—but he nevertheless felt uneasy. It all looked foreign to him.

They planned to meet in a café on a small side street where it was quiet, far from the screeching noises of life that made Januck flinch.

He stepped into the little coffee shop and his eyes met Simon's piercing gaze. Simon was sitting at a corner table with a newspaper in his hand.

"I knew you would show up some day," he said. Neither one finished the thought—provided you were still alive. Januck nodded. His mouth felt dry. He felt suddenly hot in his heavy coat. He unbuttoned it and put his hat on the chair beside him. The sun shone in through the windows, hot and demanding. Januck sweated, breathing hard.

"My sister, Magda..." He didn't know how to begin. "Do you remember, she slipped over to the other side?"

He saw Simon's face tighten, his eyes grow hard.

"I want to find her. And Ingria, my wife's sister."

Simon remembered their conversation at Mauthausen very well. He knew Januck's story up to the point when he was sent away from the camp.

But he wouldn't ask any questions. Not now. Maybe another time.

Januck drank the glass of water the waitress brought him in one draught and stared at his coffee cup doubtfully, as if afraid to touch it.

"I'm living in a care center. They gave me permission to come here," he said finally, looking up into Simon's expectant eyes. "Can you help me find them?"

Simon said he was going to make a phone call, and went out the door. Januck lifted his cup to his lips and took a hesitant sip. He hadn't had the edge of a porcelain cup against his lips in years. Coffee splashed from the cup onto the table. Januck wiped it away with his sleeve until he noticed the woman at the counter staring at him. Then he remembered, picked up his napkin and dabbed his mouth delicately with it. He glanced again at the woman, who turned her head and went back to drying glasses.

When Simon returned he was holding a slip of paper with Ingria's address. Januck thanked him, folded up the paper, and shoved it in his pocket.

"And Magda?"

"Your sister has left the country. Many people have left. And disappeared."

~

Januck went to the address written on the paper and found himself standing in front of a two-story building. He climbed the narrow wooden steps to the

167

second floor, came to the landing, knocked on the door marked number five. It was a corner room. He didn't hear anything. He waited and knocked again.

A moment later the door opened, but it wasn't Ingria; it was an older woman with a rag in her hand.

"Are you here to pick up the stuff?" she asked.

"I'm looking for Ingria Silo," Januck said.

"Yes, they're her things. Right over there," the woman said, nodding toward a cardboard box with a roll of something tied with string poking out of it. "She went to the States. Somebody was supposed to come and get this."

"When did she leave?" Januck asked.

The woman shrugged and looked at him impatiently.

"I have to get this room cleaned," she said, still more impatient, and picked up the box and handed it to him.

On the bus, Januck stared at the box in his lap, took out the roll of paper, pulled off the string, and unrolled it. He looked for a long time at the drawing—a young woman with reddish hair, one hand touching the clear water of a stream. Who was she? Some friend of Ingria's? He rolled the paper up again. On the back it said "Katherine".

NEW YORK

Mrs. Benjamin Hynes, Ingria thought as she sat in New York's Grand Central Station surrounded by the bustle of the crowd. She looked at the broad gold band on her left ring finger, as if to confirm that it was all true. "We'll have the actual wedding once we get home," Benjamin had said. So they had a short civil ceremony with Benjamin's army buddies Mark and Ted as witnesses.

A smile flickered across Ingria's lips. She could still picture that beautiful Friday afternoon when Benjamin walked up to her with one hand behind his back, refusing to show her what he was hiding there. "You should sit down in that chair first," he said, and told her to close her eyes. Then he said, "You can open them now." Benjamin was kneeling in front of her with a tiny box in his hand. "I love you. Will you be my wife?" he said, and she felt as if nothing else in the world existed, just her and Benjamin. Everything else was meaningless in that moment. He asked again. "Will you?" "Yes," she whispered, feeling as if she were gazing into the eyes of tenderness itself.

Ingria looked up at the clock. Its minute hand had advanced by one more minute. She looked at the entrance stairway, where an endless stream of men and women descended, some holding the hands of children. She turned and looked at the clock again. The hand ticked another minute.

Suddenly she felt a vague uneasiness. Benjamin had stayed behind in Vienna to wait for an army transport to Le Havre, where he would continue by transport ship to New York. Was the ship late? What was keeping him? Ingria felt her cheeks grow hot. She scanned the room around her who knows how many times, although she knew she was sitting in exactly the right place, the exact spot where they had agreed to meet when they parted in Vienna. "I'll come straight from the boat to the station and we'll take the train together to Pennsylvania," Benjamin had said at the dock. "I'll be there waiting for you," she'd answered from the train window. "And for our life together," waving to him as long as they could still see each other. Where was he? Fear started to choke her. She tried to take deep breaths, to calm down. Why hadn't he come yet? Then she saw two men in army uniforms looking at her, coming toward her. Neither one was Benjamin. One of the men was Mark, who had been a witness to their marriage. Mark was from Benjamin's hometown. They had been schoolmates. The three of them were supposed meet here and travel to Pennsylvania together. But where was Benjamin? Where?

"Hello, Ingria," Mark said, his face solemn, and Ingria knew, was somehow certain, that Benjamin wasn't coming, ever.

A moment later, she learned that the transport truck Benjamin was riding in had run over a German landmine and been blown up just before it reached Le Havre. "I'm very sorry," Mark said softly. Ingria closed her eyes. Her Benjamin hadn't come, would never come.

In a café a few minutes later with Mark sitting across from her, she said that she couldn't go to Pennsylvania, couldn't bear to meet Benjamin's parents, who are waiting there for them. Mark promised to visit them and suggested that Ingria go to the Red Cross center until everything was figured out. "There are a lot of people there whose loved ones are gone, or looking for them," he said.

~

When she first arrived at the Red Cross center, Ingria looked around and saw halls teeming with people who had lost family and friends.

She felt like a leaf falling from its tree, whirled by the wind wherever life would take her. Life wouldn't listen to her; it just whisked her wherever it wanted.

She didn't get to know the others. She kept to herself, kept drawing.

She often saw a tall man in the hallway and wondered who he was. Once, as she was walking by the open door of an office, she heard him speaking Swedish on the telephone. Someone told her he was assisting the Red Cross.

Ingria was sitting in a windowed alcove off a hallway with her sketchpad in her lap. Her newest drawing was one of Katherine. A study of her face to replace the one she'd left in Vienna. She had just finished it.

As she stood up the trees in the park outside suddenly bent at the trunk and a long, tumbling stripe of sunlight came shouting after them and she slid to the floor. She saw the man pick up her sketchpad. Rays of light tinted the hairs on his arm a bright copper. The next moment she was wrapped in a blanket of night.

MAGNOLIAS IN BLOOM

"Good morning Mrs. Hynes!" Ingria heard a happy voice said.

A woman bustled in and pulled open the drapes. It was spring, a sunny day. She had slept through the winter. She had no real memory of that time of darkness. It was as if it had shoved all the pain into its cold pit, shut everything deeper and deeper and covered it all out of sight in a blanket of snow.

She looked at the nurse.

"Perhaps today's the day to get you on your feet," the nurse said. Ingria nodded and put her feet in the slippers the woman had dropped next to the bed. She raised herself, pushing with her arms until she was upright, wobbling a little. The nurse took hold of her arm and led her to the washroom. "The magnolias are already in bloom, Mrs. Hynes", she said.

An hour later Ingria was walking on the terrace with a shawl over her shoulders, sniffing the scent of trees. She sat down in a wicker chair. She opened her sketchpad. The trees on its white pages stood up straight.

"Good morning," she heard, in a faintly accented voice as a shadow fell over her pad.

"Johan von Armenfeld," the tall man said extending his hand. He said he was an art historian. He seemed hesitant. Ingria invited him to sit down.

"I've just returned from Europe," he said. "Brussels. We're finding more stolen paintings all the time."

Ingria had read in the paper about the Monuments Men, the group of Americans who searched for lost works of art after the war.

She laid her sketchpad on a stack of books. The book at the top was Anna Karenina. She looked at the man's hands, recognized the copper-colored hairs, and said, "You looked at my drawings before you left, didn't you?"

There was something strange about the look in his eyes, but that was true of many people. The war had left a mark on their eyes, their gestures and facial expressions, that told of feelings words couldn't always convey.

"May I look at them now? Is that alright with you?" There was little smile at the edges of his mouth.

Ingria opened her sketchpad.

"My parents," she said.

And when she came to Margit: "My sister."

She also showed him her drawings of the

Waldermann family. When she got to the last page, she didn't say anything. It was a drawing of Katherine.

"A friend you lost?" Johan said.

Ingria looked into his eyes. Katherine had asked her never to tell anyone about what happened to her, and she wouldn't break a promise, wouldn't taint Katherine's memory. Johan was also quiet, and Ingria knew that they shared something they didn't have words to describe.

~

Over the following days and weeks Ingria noticed that she missed Johan's company in those moments when she wasn't needed in the office to help to translate papers and documents. Her work kept her thoughts contained, but in the evenings she often felt restless and took the subway into Manhattan. Sometimes she sat for hours in Central Park and watched the people passing. It was a river she could step into, she thought, join in life's daily rounds, move forward.

One quiet, lovely afternoon, when she was sitting in the alcove drawing after a day at work, Johan walked in carrying a package wrapped in brown paper. It was quite large, and Ingria wondered what it could be. A painting? A mirror? Johan answered her questioning look, and unwrapped it.

"What do you think of this?"

It was a painting. Magritte's *La voix du sang*. Ingria shivered and said, "I think it looks like terrible things happened in that house."

"No one knows what happened there."

"Why remind yourself of something evil?" Ingria asked.

"So it's not forgotten. So that it never happens again," Johan said with a sorrowful look. "I bought this when I was in Belgium. I hadn't been there since the war."

Ingria looked at him questioningly. The sunlight flickered through the dancing leaves of the trees outside and cast restless shadows over the little alcove.

"My job was to rescue whatever paintings I could from Hitler," Johan said slowly. "But I was ambushed in Brussels. I was in an old warehouse. There was a local gallery owner there, a friend of mine. A secret collection of modern art. It was enormously valuable—Chagall, Picasso, van Gogh... Also a few works by Magritte."

Ingria knew that these were the "degenerate" artists that Hitler hated. She nodded.

"But there were also a few classic works that Hitler wanted for his collection in Linz. I planned to take them to Germany, so I could complete my assignment."

"And what was that?" Ingria asked quietly.

"A Trojan horse; that's what we called it. You see, my friend had hidden some passports in a bronze bust. One hundred beautifully falsified passports, which I was to take over the border into Germany." Johan stared off into the distance.

Ingria waited. She didn't want to rush the ghosts of the past. But they came anyway. Came to look, came closer when you least expected them. She heard a heavy sigh.

"Just then there was machine gun fire at the door. My friend thought that I had betrayed him. He took the gun out of his pocket and aimed it at me. But the Nazis got their shots in first. I was interrogated and then let go. And I escaped here."

That look on his friend's face still tormented him. The death weighed on his conscience. He hadn't been able to save those who expected it of him. It was a burden of guilt he carried, and he had nowhere to set it down.

Ingria laid her hand on his.

One windy October evening, Ingria wrapped a wool scarf around her neck and walked to the Brooklyn Bridge. She stood at the railing and looked down at the river, dark, splashing beneath her. Water had always captivated her, water in motion, a current moving forward, going somewhere.

Mama had said that longing keeps you going.

Ingria stared at the rising swells. She felt she no longer knew how to interpret life. One minute it seemed to promise all its beauty, the next minute it plunged into darkness, the obliteration of everything.

She turned, and there was Johan, standing a short distance away, waiting.

WEST HOLLYWOOD

Magda awoke in her West Hollywood apartment, a place so small that she could fit no more than a dresser, a bed, and a small table with two wooden chairs, though no one ever sat in the second one. It was hot in her room. The air was filled with the heavy scent of jasmine. Grasshoppers buzzed outside. Magda raised herself on one elbow. The front of her nightgown was wet with sweat, sticking to her skin. Where was she? Then she remembered her dream. A nightmare.

In the dream she was standing at one end of the long entrance hall of the convent. Light slanted in from the upper window at the end of the vaulted corridor and landed on Sister Elke's bent back, and the backs of the other sisters, who were on their hands and knees scrubbing the stone floor. The revolver felt heavy in her hand, her arm hanging limp, but Wilfred, who stood beside her, said a gun was something a guard had to have. She remembers thinking how silly the nuns looked, like black starlings with their beaks to the ground. "Harder!" he commanded them, and they pressed their brushes so hard against the floor that it smashed the bristles sideways. And then she woke up.

Magda wiped the sweat from her brow with her arm. She wiped her chest, put her hand under her nightgown to wipe away the sweat from under her breasts. Her hand brushed against her nipple and she felt it harden. She closed her eyes. How long it'd been since she and Wilfred... Before she knew it, before the thought reached her consciousness, she touched the bud of it, stiff and erect. Her breath grew heavy and she squeezed the nipple between her fingers, squeezed it harder, shutting her eyes so tight it almost hurt. She put her other hand between her legs, where it was hot and wet. No, she told herself. No. She lay stiff on the bed and saw lights crossing the ceiling like years passing. Then the room was dark again. A moment later the sharp beams of light from the passing cars fell over the room again as they swept over the worn, narrow white outer wall of the apartment house with its tired trellis of grapevines.

Magda watched the movement of the lights striking the little wooden Madonna icon one moment and disappearing the next. What should she do? she wondered, her hands resting lightly on her damp chest. She couldn't really speak English, and there were very few people here who spoke German. She hadn't planned to come this far, but seeing Ingria in Manhattan in broad daylight had nearly paralyzed her. She'd been on her way to a new job at the Little Red Hen, a streetside "German" restaurant. She was just taking hold of the door handle and she glanced to the side, one hand holding her hat so the wind wouldn't blow it away, and she saw them walking hand-in-hand, Ingria and a tall man who looked at her, laughing, and Ingria smiling back at him, while the owner of the restaurant watched Magda through the glass door with a stick of salami in his hand. And she had let go of the door handle and hurried away. Heard the owner standing on the sidewalk shouting after her, "Fräulein, Fräulein!" But she didn't turn around, just held onto her hat and hurried down the windy street to the subway, the heels of her shoes clacking. When she got to Chelsea she packed her small suitcase again, stepped out of the Leo House, a hostel run by nuns, and left the life she had tried to begin behind her as she hurried across the street.

Magda sighed. A door slammed somewhere in the building. She rolled onto her side, stared at the letter from Ulka that had arrived at the poste restante a few days earlier. In the letter there were pictures of the girl. She decided to buy an album and some paste.

Magda wiped the sweat from her neck.

Will I ever be at peace? Anywhere?

IV

MISSING COLORS

Ingria woke around 2 AM needing to use the toilet. The lights of New York glowed somewhere far away, behind the heavy brocade curtains. Ingria fumbled in the dark for the table lamp's switch, finally found it, and wandered through the dim silkscreen shimmer into the bathroom. When she returned she opened the Central Park-side windows to let in some fresh night air to help her get back to sleep, and nodded off immediately.

Some hours later, she woke to the sound of a piercing scream. The Ludwig clock ticking on the night table read three minutes past five. Ingria got up from her spiral-carved four-poster bed. Just as she was closing the windows, she saw a long-haired girl run through the trees in the park like a startled deer and disappear into the darkness. Ingria froze, staring out at the dark, swaying treetops. She stood motionless, listening for a moment to the ghostly silence, broken only by the steady tick of the clock and the hum of the traffic below, then she shut the windows. But when she laid down, she heard that scream again and again. Finally she got up, walked across the floor into the living room, and switched on the lights.

It had been ages since she'd last taken *La voix du sang* off the wall, she thought as she grabbed hold of the picture frame with both hands. And why would she? She didn't have any desire to open the safe. But now she punched in the combination.

She found a few envelopes which she knew contained stock certificates and other papers she had no interest in. Johan had taken care of all that sort of thing, when he was alive. Then her eyes fell on the sketchpad. The girls. She leafed through them and stopped at the picture of the forest maidens, the maidens without faces. *They turn the light toward the darkness so people won't lose their way*, Margit had said once, long ago. *So people won't lose their way.*

~

The housekeeper, Rosina Gonzales, was sick, so Ingria made her own tea. She ate a few paper-thin cookies, spread with an equally thin layer of honey. The scream in the night troubled her. Should she call the police? Or wait until someone came to question her about it? Maybe nothing had happened. Maybe the girl had had a few too many drinks and was just fooling around with her boyfriend. If so, then a call would make her seem like a dotty old lady who calls the police every time any little thing happens, like the neighbor who summoned a patrol car when repairmen came to fix the skylights after a hailstorm. "Old people get frightened," Rosina had said, punctuating her words with swipes of the duster around the heavy frame of the Van Gogh landscape. "I'm not frightened," Ingria answered.

At exactly one o'clock the doorman called—it was the day doorman, Joseph Beal, a black man who looked about Ingria's age, but was in fact more than ten years younger.

"Mrs. von Armenfeldt, there's a letter for you."

Ingria said she would come right down for it. Although her voice was steady, her hands were shaking a little when she put down the telephone receiver.

She pulled on her dark brown fur stole— it was well along into September, after all—and pushed her feet into her gold-buckled, low-heeled walking shoes.

Before opening the apartment door she glanced in the mirror: her pale, heavily-sprayed hair was like a tidy cupola around her face. The thick layer of face powder was lined with wrinkles, like cracks in clay left dry too long, but her eyes were still a blue as deep as an autumn night sky, as if time had overlooked them. Ingria noticed her colorless lips and rummaged in her patent leather handbag for her dark lilac lipstick. It was the color she had worn for the past thirty years—lilas foncé. She had it shipped from France; the engraved gold tube arrived every three months, year after year. When Rosina shook her head and said that you could find dark lilac lipstick from closer by, Ingria had answered that she didn't want any other shade. Ingria's keen eye told her that it was the same shade her mother had worn.

When the elevator stopped at the oval, marble-floored lobby, Ingria stepped out and walked to the desk. First she saw the thick envelope, and only then Joseph, waiting behind it.

"Good afternoon, Mrs. von Armenfeldt."

"Thank you, Mr. Beal. Likewise," Ingria answered with equal courtesy, flashing an unexpected smile that instantly gave her face a surprising sweetness. Joseph knew from thirty years of experience that Mrs. von Armenfeldt didn't usually smile—especially not since her husband died. It cheered him.

"Here you go," he said, handing her the thick, dark gray envelope. There was no sender's name on it, which was unusual, and was perhaps the reason it had arrived by courier. What the letter might say, Joseph hadn't the slightest idea, but Mrs. von Armenfeldt had been very clear that whenever such an envelope arrived he should always let her know immediately, and he must never give it to her housekeeper Rosina Gonzales or put it on the counter with the other packages. There could be no mistake about this, she had stressed.

Joseph would have liked to ask Mrs. von Armenfeldt how she was doing, since her housekeeper had been out with the flu for more than a week, but he didn't dare ask. You didn't ask Mrs. von Armenfeldt such things. It was a mistake he had made once. "Where in Europe are you from?" he had asked, partly out of youthful directness, partly to show courtesy to a new tenant. Mrs. von Armenfeldt had looked at him coldly for several seconds, and he'd thought he would freeze to the core. "She's part Finnish, part Austrian, plus something else," Rosina told him later. "What else?" Joseph's raised eyebrows had asked. "Is it any of our business?" Rosina had snapped, her brown eyes flashing, and Joseph had answered that it certainly wasn't.

"Have a good afternoon, Mr. Beal," Ingria said, tightly holding the thick envelope and walking back to the elevator.

~

The first letter came on a chilly day in April. Johan was on an art-buying trip in Brussels. I held the big, heavy envelope for a moment, uncertain. It had been sent from Los Angeles. I didn't know anyone there, and there was no sender's address. I thought there must be some mistake. But it did have my name on it.

When I got home, I opened the envelope and inside was an album bound in blue. Something stirred inside me. Perhaps I already knew at some level that she existed, somewhere.

It took a moment before I was able to look at the first page.

A girl standing on a lawn, handing a doll to someone—some other person not visible in the picture.

My daughter.

THE FORGOTTEN MEN

Every day for decades they had sat down for meals at the same table, walked the same hallways to the reading room, the day room, the showers. But there were no public areas. Those three rooms seemed to form the physical boundaries of the patients' lives—a rather small group nowadays—if you didn't count the times when some of them were able to take the minibus into the city. Those trips were always guided sightseeing tours of one kind or another. Sometimes they were about architecture, sometimes statues or parks or art museums, but always chosen by Head Nurse Knauss, and the same little bus would pick them up in front of the entrance and bring them back again. It was rare to have a free day to go out on your own to explore the world outside this building hidden deep in the woods.

"He seems to have had a good day," Nurse Knauss

said to Nurse Fleimar as they passed the reading room, where Januck was just opening the newspaper. Januck read a lot. Read all the newspapers right down to the shorter articles. He knew that Simon had founded an office that tracked down Nazi war criminals. They had found the man who arrested Anne Frank, and many others. But Januck suspected that Simon had forgotten about him in the process. Either that or his sister was so well hidden in her new life that she would never be found. So he was surprised when Nurse Fleimar came to tell him that he was wanted on the telephone.

It was Simon calling. Having exchanged greetings, Simon explained that he had finally found Magda.

"I'm sorry you had to wait so long, but we lost her trail in New York."

"New York?" Januck said in amazement.

"Yes. Perhaps something happened there. She got a job in a café, but she never showed up to work there."

"I had given up hope of finding her," Januck said softly. "Where is she?"

"In a convent in California."

Januck was quiet for a long time.

"I can give you the address," Simon said, breaking the silence. "Do you have a pen and paper?"

After the call Januck went to see the care center's psychiatrist, an old man with all the memories of the war visible in his wrinkled cheeks. Januck heard that the man had survived the death camps and testified against his torturers at the Nuremberg trials. He remembered the psychiatrist from the university, an enthusiastic young man who used to attend Freud's lectures. It was all like another life now.

They had a brief chat, and the psychiatrist gave him a long look filled with understanding and said he didn't see any reason Januck couldn't travel abroad to see his only family member who had survived the war. He wrote him a prescription, too, just in case.

When Januck came out of the psychiatrist's office Nurse Knauss look at him worriedly.

"Are you absolutely sure you want to travel all that way?" she asked.

"I have to go, while I still can," Januck answered in a voice full of grief.

~

The second letter came on a lovely summer day. Johan was working at the gallery when Joseph called to tell me it had arrived.

As before, it was a large envelope that contained a blue photo album in a white box, the kind they sell at Sears and other inexpensive chain stores.

On the first page my daughter was a schoolgirl. A few pages later she was an adult, a young woman. She had a broad smile and the hope of all the future in her eyes. They were bright, happy eyes.

On the next page I learned more about her. She played tennis. Who she was playing with I don't know, because the image was cut off at the net.

All of the pictures were taken secretly, from far away.

She studied at the University of Vienna. I knew because I recognized the corner of a building in the photo. We used to ride by there on the tram. I would've liked to know what subjects she studied, but I couldn't tell from the photographs. In the last picture she was walking through a park, hand in hand with a young man.

CALIFORNIA

After morning prayers Magda often went to a nearby field to pick a variety of plants: rose petals for soap, herbs for tea, lavender, carnations, and lemon grass for fragrant oils and creams, and so on. It was one of her chores. Sometimes she saved some flowers and dried them to use as models for painted postcards, or to make bookmarks. Twinflowers and forget-me-nots were best for those.

As she picked some salvia, Magda felt it was going to be an especially hot day. The sun was already high in the sky, bright and sharp. Soon it's yellow sphere would be radiating its heat down on her head from a cloudless sky. The heat didn't used to bother her as much, but she was sixty-six now, and easily tired. She decided to use the salvia to make a balm for sunburn.

Looking up, she saw someone emerge from a grove of mandarin trees and walk through a field of cowpeas, straight toward her. She squinted, unable to make out the man's face, shaded by the brim of his hat in the bright sunlight.

She stood waiting with her basket over her arm. Then she heard a long, low whistle floating over the field, like a cold wind that went right through her. She didn't move.

"You found me," she said as her brother strode up to her, as if there had never been any years between them. "All the way out here." The corners of her mouth turned up in a small, bitter smile.

Januck felt a trickle of sweat run down his neck. He longed for cool shade. To be under the orange and lemon trees.

"Let's go over there," Magda said, nodding in the direction of his thoughts.

They sat down on two wobbly wooden chairs.

Januck looked around at the landscape, at a tractor left in a field of sweet potatoes, the citrus grove.

The sun through the branches flickered over his face, intermittently blinding him with its light.

He was suddenly painfully aware of the two them, sitting under an orange tree in this faraway landscape. He looked at the woman beside him, her aged face, and felt the distant approach of a sudden warmth of love flooding deep within him for his sister, who once long ago came stomping across the room toward him on her pudgy child's feet.

Januck said softly, "I understand that you want to be left in peace."

They sat side by side and gazed at the tranquil countryside, everything shimmering with the promise of heat.

"You know, Magda, I never cease to be surprised at people's ability to explain their own actions—to themselves—no matter what bad things they've done."

"Like us," Magda said.

"Yes," Januck whispered, his voice choked.

"I trust in the mercy of God," Magda murmured.

Januck picked up a dry stick and drew meandering lines in the sand with it.

Magda watched, following its pattern of tendrils. Abruptly, he stopped drawing and took hold of the stick with both hands as if to test its strength. Then there was a snap, and the stick broke. Magda startled.

"Life has no meaning without love. You might as well be dead. Your life dries up, like this stick. I loved Margit."

He threw the pieces of the stick on the ground and put his face in his hands. His body shook with anguish, with all the love that was lost.

"I thought everything I did was right. But how could I know what was right?" Januck said, wiping his eyes on his sleeve.

"You couldn't," Magda said quietly. "No one could."

"No one has the final answer," Januck said. "That's just how it is."

Magda wrapped an arm around his stooped

shoulders and said, "Would you like to come in and eat with us?"

~

I waited a long time for the next album to arrive. I was starting to think there would be no more pictures coming. Then one day in December I was coming back from shopping—I had been buying some Christmas ornaments—and as I was shaking the sleet from my umbrella, I heard Joseph's greeting, and when I turned around I saw that he was holding a large, thick, gray envelope.

I put it in my purse and turned on my heel, because my husband was home. I walked back out into the driving sleet and hurried to a nearby café.

I saw her now a grown woman. A mother. A chubby-cheeked little boy in a stroller. I had become a grandmother.

It was the best Christmas present I ever received.

RETURN TO THE LIFE OF THE FLESH

Not long after her brother came to visit, Magda walked out of the gates of the convent carrying nothing but a small brown suitcase with her few belongings and boarded a bus for Los Angeles. When she arrived she bought a few essential clothes on sale and found a cheap motel on Sunset Boulevard. Two days later she got a job as a women's washroom attendant in a restaurant and started saving up her tips, thinking she would soon move into an apartment.

The restaurant was one of those large woodframe places that had survived for decades offering simple food. The owner, Mr. Kern, hadn't spent any money to speak of maintaining the place, but something about its faded 1940s charm made it a favorite among the younger generation of Hollywood film people.

Ed Kern was a rather tall, broad-shouldered man in his 70s who looked like a B movie actor. His brown, film noir eyes bespoke a weary, sorrowful world. Kern had noticed Magda's accent, but he didn't ask for her papers any more than he had asked his Mexican errand boys.

When the older woman in a blue blouse and black, calf-length skirt had appeared asking for work two weeks earlier, he'd thought that she was too old to be a waitress, but when she looked in his eyes and asked him, "Is there any work at all?" he invented the washroom attendant's position for her— a job you generally only saw in the better hotel restaurants and nightclubs. And it didn't require any experience.

"What kind of work have you done before?" he had asked her, out of mere curiosity. And she had answered, in a choked voice, "All kinds. I was at a convent."

Kern was used to hearing all sorts of stories from more or less legal job applicants to explain a lack of references, been witness to all sorts of touching pleas, but this one took the cake.

"Everybody's welcome at my church," he'd said, gazing down at her.

~

On her first evening, Kern had given her basic instructions and disappeared up the worn, red-carpeted staircase.

Magda spread a large pink napkin on the little washroom table, placed the tip basket on it, and arranged the pink hand towels into neat stacks so as to easily hand them to customers after they washed their hands. A spritz of cheap perfume or hairspray cost 25 cents each; the price was posted on the wall above the table.

Customers usually left a dollar bill in the basket. After the restaurant closed, Magda scrubbed away various splashes and excretions from the perfume-permeated room.

The next day, Kern came downstairs just before the restaurant opened. Magda was polishing the mirror.

"Looks good," Kern said glancing around the room, which was cozy as a dollhouse with Magda's wool coat hanging homey on the wall from a wire hanger, and a bunch of artificial flowers in a cheap porcelain vase and a cute little gold-colored tip basket on the table.

Magda nodded and said, "Thank you, Mr. Kern."

He flashed a broad smile revealing yellow false teeth. "Call me Eddy."

Magda nodded and continued polishing the mirror, and before she knew it, Eddy had turned and reached out his hand and squeezed her right breast. It didn't last long. It was as if he we're quickly squeezing an air pump.

When she saw him later, at closing time, he was deep in conversation with the cook and head waiter, and took no notice of her leaving.

The next night, when Eddy's brown, wide-legged trousers came flapping down the stairs, Magda was on her guard. She sat down on the wooden chair between the table and the toilet stall.

"Ah! I see everything is in order here."

Magda nodded.

"I haven't yet had a chance to introduce you to the staff," Eddy said. "Why don't you come upstairs with me before the customers start arriving. By the way, we're expecting an engagement party this evening. Thirty people. Should be pretty busy."

Magda got up and followed him, but he stopped at the foot of the stairs, and so did she. Then he turned around and reached out a hand, and Magda closed her eyes. As his hand squeezed her breast, she felt intoxicated, as if she herself was a flower thick-scented with jasmine.

～

Magda felt uneasy thinking about Eddy. He stayed away for a few days, and every time she heard steps on the stairs she expected to see his brown, pressed trousers flap into view. I'm too old for this sort of thing, she thought as she wiped a toilet lid and picked up her scrub brush. The other stalls were clean but she had noticed a dried splash of yellow on this one and had just given it a scrub. Then she felt a hand on her hip and Eddy pressed tight against her from behind.

"A sweet ass. Round as a peach," he said.

Magda waited with the scrub brush in her hand for his next move. She felt his hand slip expertly under her skirt and into her panties, so smooth she hardly noticed what was happening. His other hand held her tight around the waist and—as she guessed he would—fumbled with his fly.

"We have nothing to worry about," he mumbled. "Not nowadays."

Magda let the brush fall from her hand to the floor and held onto the rusty pipes above the toilet with both hands. She was amazed at how wet she was.

As she walked home that night, listening to the cicadas singing in the bushes along the sidewalk, she felt bewildered. Somebody's mistress? Is that what was happening? No. She wouldn't allow it. Or his wife? He was considerably older than her, but what did it matter? He seemed virile enough, at least. Yes, she wanted to be Eddy's wife. Magda smiled to herself, and at the people passing. What's done is done, she said to herself, and felt alive, like an apple fresh bitten by the frost.

~

I put on Chopin's fourth ballade—my mother's favorite—and poured myself some cognac. Only then did I open the album on the living room table.

The boy looked happy and healthy. It thrilled me. He walked down the street, holding his mother's hand. In the next picture they were looking at something. He was pointing at something. His little mouth was open, like the letter O.

There were lots of photos of them together. The boy's father had been cut away. It was just mother and son.

In the next picture he was a teenager.

In the last one, he was in baggy shorts and a numbered jersey. He was standing in a corner bouncing a ball. He had an intense look of concentration on his face.

V

THE BOY, 2004

His cheekbones seemed sharper than before, Ingria thought, turning to the next page of the photo album. And there was a crease of worry between his mother's eyes now. In the next picture he was being handed a prize, or perhaps a diploma. The picture was taken in an auditorium. Maybe at school? In any case, her daughter was smiling in that one. A beautiful smile, a little shy, as if she'd been a bit dazzled by the attention. Then the pictures of her stopped, and pictures of the boy continued. He grew much taller in the last years. His hair was in a bowl cut, and he was holding something black, an instrument case. His face had a serious expression, as he opened a heavy door. Where was he going? What instrument did he play? The clarinet? Perhaps the flute? He had Hans's bright, watchful eyes. Clear and searching.

Ingria's heart started to pound fast, like a bird's. She braced herself on a corner of the table and stood up.

She got a tumbler from the glass cabinet and poured herself some cognac. It burned her mouth as she took a sip and sat down at the table again.

When she got to the last page the afternoon shadows had reached the corners of the room.

She put the album in its white box and went to the utility room. The narrow window was covered in rough, thick gold glass that cast a yellow glow over the dim room. The walls were lined with shelves and cabinets that gaped empty and the only piece of furniture was a rococo armchair with its seat missing, standing in front of the unused sink. The room hadn't been used for many years, and Rosina had no reason to go in there.

Ingria reached behind the curtain, felt around on the wall, and found a bulge under the wallpaper. She pulled a metal key out from under the paper, then put the key into the lock she'd had installed on the cupboard, and opened the door. She placed the box on the second highest shelf next to another box exactly like it. There were three more on the shelf above. She looked at them for a moment—her past, packaged and hidden away—and then she locked the cabinet.

For a moment she didn't move, just hung her head. She stared at the yellow light on her hands, that crisscross of veins, like little rivers on a map.

JANUCK AND HANS

In his room at the care center, Januck had his own small television with antennas poking out that he had to adjust now and then because the picture was faint, occasionally fading to gray static. He kept the sound turned low, because some of the patients couldn't withstand the outside world.

Januck had been indoors all day because of the pouring rain. Now his eyes were fixed on the television screen. A mound of upturned earth, and beside it a pit filled with rainwater. An excavator was parked next to the mound. In the foreground stood a young man in a raincoat.

"Several days after a crew began excavating the site you see behind me for a new shopping center, they made a shocking discovery," he said. "Excavator operator Rudolf Geier was the first to notice bones floating in this pit, when he was moving an excavator to higher ground following a heavy rain. Since then a flood of investigators and forensics experts have been to the site, because more bones have been found, and they all appear to be the remains of teenage girls. Locals here know that there was once a clock factory nearby, operated by the Nazis during the war, where girls and young women worked. The foundations of the factory are still intact, and locals speculate that the building was destroyed by a bomb. That would not, however, explain the mass graves that have just been found."

A clock factory? Januck felt his breath speed up. Magda. And the soldier. Wilfred. *My uncle Reinhard has a clock factory.*

Januck looked at the girl with the mahogany hair, one of the drawings Ingria had left behind. He took it down from the wall. The girl's eyes looked secretive, happy, like someone hiding the most beautiful thing she's ever found in her whole life. Maybe she was in love... Like Margit was in love with him.

It's raining. Almost a torrent. He stands at the edge of the pit with a shovel in his hand. Looks down. They're not dead. He sees a hand move, reaching toward him. Margit. He jumps into the pit, heaves the sopping sand away. He takes hold of the hand. Margit, Margit, he shouts, his lungs nearly tearing open... Then his voice is drowned in the mud.

Januck heard Simon's voice from some past moment, some other place. It said,

Those who lose hope die.

The hand stops. He grabs it. It isn't Margit's hand. It's still warm.

The static on the television screen cleared for a moment, then the picture disappeared again. He had to go there. Januck turned off the television and walked out of the room. He stopped at Nurse Fleimar's station and asked to go out for the afternoon.

~

At the wooded intersection behind the care center, Januck caught a bus that took him to the place. When he arrived, it was swarming with reporters, including foreign television crews. Local people seemed to have nearly disappeared, everyone indoors. And the locals who were out on the street and in the shops taking care of daily errands had stony looks on their faces.

As he made his way through the swarm of people, Januck looked like a lost old man, holding a drawing of an attractive young woman in a clear plastic sleeve. Rachel Winter, a young American journalist, noticed him.

"Excuse me sir, who you looking for?" she asked. A plastic pocket with a press picture ID hung from a lanyard around her neck.

Januck looked at the bright-eyed woman, water dripping from the brim of her rain hat onto her nose.

"A girl who disappeared during the war," Januck

said hesitantly. Then he noticed that the cameraman was filming them, and he froze.

"Who was she?" the woman asked.

Januck shook his head, not knowing what to say.

"Do you have missing relatives?" she said, attempting another angle.

Januck didn't answer; he just looked at the ground.

"Do you have any idea what might've happened here during the war?"

Januck looked at her and mumbled, "Maybe they'll find faces for them some day."

He took a few steps, then turned and said, "My wife and her parents were killed in a concentration camp. So were my own parents."

Rachel Winter looked at him as he walked away.

~

Before leaving the village Januck stopped in at a local tavern. He was cold. He ordered a warm pastry and a cup of tea. There was a man sitting next to him at the bar who had lost one hand. Januck surmised that he was old enough to have served in the war, at least toward the end.

Hans was trying to get his lunch eaten as quickly as possible, taking quick sips from a stein of beer.

"It's as if no one knows anything," Januck said. "It must have been so horrible that people still can't talk about it. Shooting young girls."

"Not everyone was on the same side back then,"

Hans said, just as his eyes fell on the auburn-haired girl in the portrait, gazing out through the rain-drenched plastic film.

"Was she a relative of yours?" Hans asked, nodding toward the picture and shoveling food into his mouth.

"No."

"The war was a long time ago. They're already dead, almost all of them," Hans said, his face taciturn.

"Who?"

"The guilty ones."

"That doesn't ease the pain of their loved ones."

"We all lost something," Hans said softly.

He finished his meal and wiped his mouth with his napkin.

"Müller. Franz Müller shot them. If that's any help. He's dead, too."

PAGES OF MEMORIES

Magda lay on the double bed. She had thrown off the blanket. The windows were open. There was a hum of cicadas outside. The heat was as unmoving as it was on the day when Eddy sat down on the edge of the bed and said, "Didn't you miss men when you were in the convent?" They had been "an item", as Eddy put it, for several months. She looked at Eddy's rounded back, like the back of a lean, crouching animal, his vertebrae visible as he bent over to put on his socks. She had studied this man, his back with its dark hairs, his flabby stomach. The furrowed creases on the back of his neck. The gray hair that would soon replace all the brown, thin and tousled. The brown skin of his scalp, smooth as a tide-worn stone.

What had she said in reply? Magda rolled onto her side and stared at the wall. She couldn't remember.

All she could remember was his bent back. The trail of vertebrae that ran down it like camel tracks through a desert.

Another, similar night, years later, Eddy said, "I'm happy with you. If I hadn't met you I would never have experienced this."

Magda closed her eyes for a moment and reached toward the empty pillow beside her, then opened her eyes again; Eddy's small brown crucifix hung on the wall, and next to it an oval landscape painting of a snowy mountain peak against a blue sky. It was inscribed "Austria". She'd bought it at a yard sale, perhaps in some moment of nostalgia. Magda's gaze wandered to the envelope that lay leaning against the mirror on top of the bureau. Inside it was the notice of her brother's death. She had called the care center. They told her that Januck had fallen peacefully asleep in a chair in the garden. "He had a gentle passing," the nurse had said in a soft voice. "The sun was just peeping out after a rain." Magda had let out a little sob and ended the call. A mass grave. It had been on the news.

Tomorrow she would send the last photographs of the boy, and include his name and address.

She turned onto her back, heard to the sound of an approaching helicopter. They were searching for someone again. A bright light swept over the ceiling.

ON THE SHORES OF DREAMS

Ingria had taken her sleeping pill. Her hand rested on the remote control. She recognized the voice of Rachel Winter, the television reporter, distant, from across the sea.

"The discovery of the girls' mass grave has shocked both local residents and others around the world. Who the girls were, and what happened here, are questions still lingering in many minds. Here on my right there was at one time a building. That is known for certain because the foundations can still be seen, but it was apparently destroyed in a bombing—or bombed on purpose when it was abandoned. The lack of information about family members who disappeared during the war still torments their descendants. The question of the identity of the girls in the mass graves may perhaps remain one of those painful riddles…"

Ingria opened her eyes and saw the rain-soaked meadow on the television. There were flowers growing here and there, bluebells… and mountain anemones… the spring water felt cool on her hand. Refreshing.

At the spring in Ingria's dreams, she turned, saw the bending stalks of grass… She shouted, shouted into the darkness, and then she woke up and recognized the empty room around her. Heard the tick of the Ludwig clock.

It was 20 minutes to midnight.

She got up and went into the living room in her long night gown, her hair standing up in tangled spikes, stiff from yesterday's hairspray.

She took *La voix du sang* down from the wall and laid it on the sofa. Removed the old yellow sketchpad from among the stacked documents and stock certificates in the safe and walked with it to the dining room, where she switched on the lights and set the pad on the table. Then she rummaged in the utility room for a while until she found her old box of chalk pastels.

She sat down at the long dining room table and stared at the cover of her sketchpad, felt her muscles tense… and opened it.

There was the broad face of Bozka, the first to run, shouting, "Run to the forest!". And there was Katherine, her look of horror when she saw the men, the alcohol gleam in their eyes as they hungrily groped for the girls, lunging after their starved bodies. Ingria heard the first shot, saw Iwona fall, then Eliza and the others, their pale, narrow backs falling among the dark trunks of the trees. "Stop!" echoing over everything. Shouts and gunshots reverberating in the treetops, among the twisted branches, until they disappeared into the quiet of the sky.

Ingria looked down at the smudged pastel box, and through it into the night when she lay awake with the other girls and they heard the car doors opening outside. A stranger's voice giving orders to hurry. The sharp clang of shovels passed around, the thud of running footsteps.

"They're burying them," one of the girls whispered in the darkness.

Ingria picked up a piece of chalk and drew the first line of Bozka's cheek.

When the first pale ray of sunlight penetrated the room, Ingria had drawn all of them. Her knuckles ached, her fingers were stiff and covered in chalk.

She put the drawing in an envelope and walked to the entryway. She took her mink coat from its hanger, pulled it on over her nightgown, and pressed the button on the private elevator.

"Good morning, Mrs. von Armenfeldt," Joseph said with a sunny smile, though his heart hurt to see the woman growing ever frailer, the protruding joints of her fingers, the blue veins on her hands.

"How can I help you?"

The woman handed him a large envelope.

"I need your assistance, Mr. Beal," she began. Joseph listened attentively. It was a confidential matter. He understood. He assured her that he was only too happy to help. He looked at the envelope. It was addressed in elegant cursive to reporter Rachel Winter.

NEW YORK, 2004

As Magda walked down East 85th Street, golden afternoon sunlight flickered in the leaves of linden trees stirred by a gentle wind. It reminded her of some lost feeling she had in Vienna. A lightness. Was it when she and Ingria rode the Ferris wheel at Prater? Ingria felt dizzy when they reached the top, but Magda had craned to look over the edge at the world beneath them and screeched with joy, all around them the rushing sky, the land, the tiny houses of the city. She had been filled with a hope for future life that felt so intoxicating and exciting that she almost felt she would burst, her cheeks hot and red. Life had something thrilling to offer, at that moment she had been absolutely certain of it.

How sweet and innocent everything was then. The rotating Ferris wheel, the music as entrancing as young love. Even that experience had been granted to her. But also everything else. The kind of life she hadn't planned.

Magda turned at the corner and looked up, and she saw Ingria standing at the window, peering out between the curtains, waiting.

Magda raised her hand slightly and waved to her.

EVERYTHING I KNOW

Ingria climbed the steps of the Musikverein carrying the concert program for Mahler's sixth Symphony. The evening was cool and she pulled her mink coat tighter around her as she lifted the hem of her blue evening gown. There was a pink hint of excitement in her cheeks. With every step she thought of the young man somewhere in this enormous building preparing himself for the concert. And she knew that the only thing that hadn't been destroyed by time, or by anyone, or any thing, was what she was feeling at that moment.

As she stepped into the majestic and beautiful Golden Hall filled with murmuring concertgoers, a feeling of peace descended upon her.

The gilded room quieted, the murmuring stopped, and a side door open. The members of the orchestra arrived one by one, the men in tails, the women in black gowns. She watched each one of them. She felt her heartbeat rise to a rapid patter that rang in her ears, and she almost felt faint. Then she saw a young man come through the door with a clarinet in his hand and take his place. He shook his head lightly to toss his hair from his face and smiled to himself. Florian.

Ingria couldn't take her eyes off him. She followed Florian's every movement, his every gesture and expression, as if time had come to a stop, as if she had to be present in its every fleeting second.

Meritta Koivisto (Veilleux) is a Finnish novelist with an international background, having spent significant time in Stockholm and Los Angeles. With seven published books in Europe, she is also a screenwriter, playwright, and director who has garnered international awards and recognition in both the US and Europe.

Among her notable achievements, her short film *Balthazar's Funeral* was a contender for the Academy of Motion Picture Arts and Sciences Awards, and her American play *Privacy* was a Top 10 Finalist at the New Century Writer Awards, supported by Francis Ford Coppola's Zoetrope. Additionally, her acclaimed short film *Wrestling With A Bee* was broadcast by ARTE Cinema.

Koivisto's gently ironic novel *The London Lover* is currently being adapted into a film in the UK, for which she wrote the screenplay. The novel is set to be published in the US in 2025.

In recent years, she has penned a highly popular Nordic noir thriller series based in Stockholm, available in audio and e-book formats for the Swedish audiobook and streaming company Storytel. The first bestselling part of the series, *The Affinity*, will launch in English in 2024. She is currently working on the fourth instalment of the series.

Made in United States
North Haven, CT
03 December 2024

61549227R00143